I0742990

Hotel

Also by RIK LONSDALE

Novel
Water and Blood

Collection
Morsels of Life

Links

www.riklonsdale.com

linktr.ee/riklonsdale

HOTEL

Rik Lonsdale

Cover design

Cover design by Rik Lonsdale

AI Statement

No artificial intelligence software has been used in the creation of any part of this book.

Copyright © 2024 by Rik Lonsdale
www.riklonsdale.com
All Rights Reserved.

No part of this book may be used or reproduced by any means, graphic, electronic, or mechanical, including photocopying, recording, taping, or by any information storage retrieval system, without the written permission of the publisher except in the case of brief quotations embodied in critical articles and reviews.

This is a work of fiction. Names, characters, places, and incidents are the product of the author's imagination. Any resemblance to actual persons, living or dead, events, or locales is entirely coincidental.

ISBN 978-1-7392823-4-9 Paperback
ISBN 978-1-7392823-5-6 E-book

FOME

Chapter 1

I KNOW I am judged when I arrive at reception. A single, measured, glance from the man behind the polished satinwood counter, followed by the minutest of pauses before he speaks, and he sees the impostor I know myself to be. He raises an eyebrow, almost imperceptibly, when I give my name, and glances down at his computer to confirm my booking.

'One moment, sir,' he says. 'I'm paging Banks, he'll be here shortly.'

'Who's Banks?' I say.

'Banks is the suite's butler, sir. He'll take your luggage and unpack for you.' This accompanied by a swift glance at my fifteen-year-old "wheely".

'Then he'll introduce you to the suite's facilities and ask about your personal preferences regarding service, sir.' The pause between "service" and "sir" fractionally longer than it might be. It feels like a slight. I ignore it and hear a cough behind me.

I turn to be greeted by my name formed as a question.

'I've been expecting you, sir. I'm Banks, your butler for your stay, may I take your case?'

He bends to take the handle. I almost say no, in the polite way you do when you don't need any help, but hold myself in check. This is his job. I murmur a 'Thank you, Banks,' and follow him to the elevator. He's about fifty, younger than I. He wears a crisp white shirt and tie beneath a waistcoat and black jacket and trousers. Polished patent shoes complete the ensemble, not a uniform, but clearly an employee.

Banks is efficient and attentive. He introduces all the suite's accoutrements and its technology. He pays particular attention to the paging system while telling me he's available twenty-four hours a day for the most minor of eventualities. He unpacks my case with reverence, despite the undoubted shabbiness of its contents compared to previous occupants. He asks if I need anything pressing for the evening. I almost say no but ask him to iron the better of my two shirts. I have a couple of hours to spare so I take a stroll along the embankment and have coffee in the hotel lounge. There's plenty of time to change before my guest's arrival.

She's late. I look at my watch again and pace the room. I stand and stare out of the window, across the Thames, not seeing the boats on the river, not seeing the London Eye, not seeing the Millennium Bridge, not seeing the skyscrapers on the south bank. All I see is an image of home; small, quiet, and rural. Not quite the opposite of where I stand; this suite at the Corcorran, one of London's most prestigious hotels, can't be described as noisy. Even staff in the corridors speak quietly, their voices hushed further by thick Wilton carpet.

By the hotel's standards this is a modest suite, but a single night costs more than a year's property tax on my own home. Standing here, I know I am a fake, I don't belong, it's not my style. During the six weeks since I booked this suite, I've almost cancelled it three times, my mouse pointer hovering over the button. But I didn't, I let the booking stand and travelled into central London to occupy this opulent space for a scant twenty-four hours. I don't know if I'll ever want to do it again. I turn from the window.

A small dining table is positioned so occupants can take in the view as they eat; next to it stands an ice bucket containing a bottle of Taittinger. At home I could have bought a Krug, perhaps even a

Kristal, for the same amount the hotel charges, but I never would. It always seems an excessive indulgence, champagne. I'm not sure why I ordered it. I guess I want to impress my guest, but I don't know why, I have nothing to prove.

I sit on the sofa, comfortable, clean, but somehow sterile, like all the furnishings. Well designed, high quality, chairs, desk, units, in classic styles and unknowable vintage, no scratches or marks on any of it. All top quality, but somehow exudes a sense of the impersonal; furniture meant to impress, not to be lived with.

I decide to open the champagne. Either she'll arrive soon or not at all, either way it will make no difference. I go to pick up the bottle, then stop and pick up the hotel phone instead. Banks answers immediately.

'I'd like the champagne opening, Banks,' I say.

'Yes, sir. I'll be there in a moment.'

He knocks on the door and waits to be summoned before entering.

'There's no sign of my guest, I take it?' I say as Banks eases the cork from the Taittinger and pours a glass.

'Not as yet, sir,' he says, delivering the glass on a small silver tray to the occasional table by the chair I occupy. 'As you instructed, I shall let you know as soon as she arrives. Will there be anything else, sir?'

'No, you can go Banks.'

'Thank you, sir.'

And he leaves. He makes no sound as he moves. The click of the door barely audible. If she doesn't arrive in the next ten minutes, I'll order dinner without her, I decide.

As I drink the most expensive champagne I've ever bought; I sit and stare at the lights on the big wheel of the Eye and wonder why they had ever bothered to build it. The answer is money, of course. British Airways' involvement meant the early rides on the glorified Ferris wheel were booked as "flights", despite no flying taking place. I've never been on it, and don't see the need to either. I get up and walk to the window again in time to see a black limousine disappear beneath the awning of the hotel.

I'm swirling the dregs of the first glass around when the phone blips at me. It's a message from Banks.

- Your guest has arrived. Shall I bring her straight up, or would a slight delay be in order?

Do I want to stoop to playing games? No, I don't think I do.

- Bring her straight up.

I down the remnants of the glass.

I TOLD SERGEI about the punter. I had to. He gets vengeful if you keep secrets from him. The clients I usually get in upmarket hotels are middle aged men in finance or something who make outrageous demands even before I get to the job. But this guy seems to be different. For one thing, he's a lot older than my usual. I don't mind. I don't care how old they are. Actually, that's not true, I do care. The older the better really, they get worn out sooner and I can get on with my life. If they're too young, they just want to start over again.

Anyway, I get a call from this bloke who tells me he's seen my profile and he'd like to book me. That was six weeks ago. It's a lot longer notice than I usually get so I was a bit suspicious. I wondered what was going on with him, so I asked, and he told me straight it was the only night he could book the suite he wanted at the hotel. When I told him there were plenty of hotels, he said he wanted this one because it looked over the river and he thought we could have dinner together and would that be all right with me and did I have any special dietary things or allergies. I almost laughed, but I didn't because he sounded serious about it. I told him I'd be happy to have dinner with him as long as he was paying. He said he'd already assumed he would be, so I figured he understood the game.

Sergei asked all sorts of questions about him. I

think he was wondering if he could be a mark for his blackmail business, but I didn't have a lot to tell him. Even so I think Sergei checked him out because he told me he'd get Jamie to drive me over and pick me up, but he wouldn't be hanging about waiting for me. I guess my man can't be super wealthy. Maybe not, but a suite at the Corcorran would set him back a couple of grand a night at least. Which meant there should be a decent tip on top of the fee, and that would be for me. Well, mostly for me. Sergei is bound to ask, and he has an uncanny way of knowing if I'm lying. He's a bastard he is. But he's useful. I've had a bit of trouble in the past from punters, and Sergei makes sure it doesn't happen.

One guy did hurt me once. Sergei took pictures of his injuries. If he thinks anyone might try the same on one of us girls, he makes sure they see what he's capable of. The guy wasn't hospitalised for too long.

Jamie arrives in the Merc to pick me up. It's swanky, but not the swankiest of Sergei's cars. If he wanted to impress it would be the Bentley. But it's doubtful the john will see it, so it doesn't matter. Jamie says he'll drop me at the main entrance; he's had a word with front desk, so I'm expected. He's a bit of an arsehole is Jamie, but he never asks me any daft questions about the gig, not like Ralph. I'm glad it wasn't Ralph doing the driving. He always has a lecherous smirk about him.

Jamie does the gentlemanly thing, picks up my case, and puts it in the boot, then opens the back door for me to get in. I'm wearing my killer heels and it's a bit of a hobble, so he puts his arm out for me. Maybe he's not such an arse; I'm wearing a plunge top too, but Jamie looks up at the sky and murmurs something about the weather. Ralph would have leered down my top, tried to make me feel awkward.

Jamie gets in the front, and we set off across town. It should only take us fifteen minutes, but there's been an accident at Piccadilly Circus so we get diverted. And the traffic soon builds up. We're going to be late. I hate being late. I'm never late. I can feel myself getting annoyed. I'm angry with Jamie, with London, with the Police. I tell myself I have to calm down, there isn't anything I can do about it. And I don't want to meet my client in a temper, do I? If he gets a whiff of how temperamental I can be and decides he's changed his mind, Sergei isn't going to be pleased. I take a couple of deep breaths while Jamie does his best with the traffic. I'm always a bit nervous before I meet a client, especially a new one. I guess it's a bit like stage fright. That's what I am really. An actor, I play whatever part will fulfil the clients demands. I get well paid for it too, a lot more than most actors, except the famous ones.

Finally, we're out of the traffic and along The Embankment, then slipping under the Corcorran's massive awning. I've been here before, but only once or twice. And my customers have never had a suite before, so I regard it as a bit of a promotion. I added a bit to my fee when we discussed it. He didn't seem to care, not like some of them, who want all the extras for free. I figure if this guy wants any extras he'll be happy to pay.

I stay in the back seat and wait for Jamie to open the door. He's put his chauffeur's cap on and I almost laugh, but stop myself. The doorman says, 'good evening, madam,' and opens the hotel door for me. Jamie gets my case out of the boot and the doorman signals a porter who quickly collects it. I turn to Jamie and say 'That will be all, James. You may go.' Jamie says, 'Thank you, ma'am.' And gets back in the car. We all take it very seriously, this acting lark, but we all know why I'm really here. Right down to the bell boy. And a bit of me hates it. But The Corcorran Hotel is so swanky. I'd never pay to stay here, costs a bomb. Probably because it absolutely is the best hotel in London, and it's on the river.

In the foyer, before I get to reception, the porter gets stopped by a bloke in a suit. I think he might be the punter, but he looks too young, and acts too distant.

'I'll take madam's case,' he says.

The porter hands it over, but I can see he's a bit pissed off. He's not going to get a tip, is he? He wouldn't have got one anyway. I don't tip hotel staff; they all know why I'm here. If they treat me right, I'll smile at them; that should be reward enough. He's talking to me, now, is the suit.

'Good evening, madam, I'm Banks, Mr. Wainwright's butler. He has asked me to take you directly to his suite. If you'll come this way.'

He's got his own butler. I should have charged him more. Maybe I'll ask him, at the right time, for a bit extra, give him some sort of sob story. Some of the older guys go for that.

Chapter 2

She's shorter than I imagined. It's hard to tell from photos. A smidge taller than Banks's shoulder, but he's over six feet, so about five feet five or six, I guess; less the heels of course.

'Come in,' I say. 'It's Georgia, isn't it? I'm Andrew. Andrew Wainwright.' I put out my hand.

As she steps forward, I catch a whiff of her perfume. It isn't a sweet, flowery sort of smell, but something deeper, darker, more subtle. I can't help but inhale it as she takes my hand.

I shake her neat and well-manicured hand. The nail polish matches the vivid red of her lipstick. The way she takes my hand and looks me in the eye at the same time is confident, self-assured.

'Pleased to meet you, Andrew,' she says. Her voice at odds with her size, a contralto maybe, though of course she doesn't sing her greeting. And a little raspiness in her voice. I wonder if she smokes, though I can't smell any sign of tobacco.

Her eyes have a hint of grey in the blue I hadn't seen in the photos. But that doesn't bother me. Undoubtedly she is beautiful. To my eye, anyway. That's why I chose her I suppose. It wouldn't have made sense to choose someone I found unattractive.

I hear Banks give a small cough, our agreed signal he wished to speak but not interrupt. I glance at him, standing behind Georgia. He holds her small case and looks down at it. I freeze for a moment or two before understanding.

'Banks, would you take Miss Stratton's case to the bedroom.'

'Yes, sir. Would Miss Stratton like me to unpack for her?'

There's a glimmer of panic and a quick shake of her head.

'No Banks, just put it on the stand,' I say.

Banks goes to the bedroom and I am dumbstruck, don't know what to say. 'Thank you for coming,' I eventually say into the growing silence, and regret the choice of words as I see the corners of her mouth briefly begin a smile before she gets them under control.

'My pleasure,' she says. Is that an almost

raised eyebrow, a hint at irony?

Then Banks is back in the room. I don't want him here, but he knows already.

'Will that be all, sir,' he says.

'Yes, Banks, I think so, except for dinner.'

'There are menus on the table, sir. If you let me know when you're ready, I'll return and take your orders.'

'Thank you, Banks.' And he slides out of the suite with barely a sound.

'Would you like champagne, Georgia? Or would you like to freshen up?'

She glances at the Taittinger. I can't tell if it's something she's used to or not. 'I don't usually drink when I'm… visiting. But a small glass of champagne would be lovely,' she says. 'And I would like to freshen up before dinner. Would you mind pouring me a glass while I pop to the bathroom?' And she goes to the bedroom, closing the door behind her.

I figure she'll check me out while she's in there. Have a look at my stuff, make sure I'm good for the money. She won't find a lot. I'm not staying much longer than she is. And none of my things are expensive. I don't buy expensive designer clothes. I don't see the need. I'm not trying to impress anyone. Or am I? Am I trying to impress Georgia? Is that why I ordered champagne? So she won't see me as merely another "client". Christ, it's such an ugly word, but I guess that's what I am, her client.

She comes back in, and I don't know what to say to her, so I just give her the champagne. And she takes it.

Banks knocks on the door, waits for a response, opens it and steps in ahead of me. I think he's being rude until he announces my arrival.

'Miss Stratton, to see you, sir,' he says, stepping aside to let me walk in, and I see the man for the first time. He told me he was seventy when he made the booking and I expect some old crusty, but he's well turned out. He's nailed the smart/casual look, and his grey hair is short and tidy. I thought he might be a fatty. They sometimes go for us smaller girls; they like to crush us. Well, that's my experience anyway. I've put a weight limit on it now. But this guy isn't fat. He's slim, neat, clean. Which is only polite really. And pretty much what I expect.

He calls me by my name and puts his hand out to shake, as if I'm a bloke, or a friend. I'm a bit surprised, but don't show it of course. They usually go in for a clinch straight away.

He looks at me and I can tell he likes what he sees. Then the butler wants to unpack my case. I almost die of panic. I mean, well, I've brought along a few things with me, haven't I. You never know what someone might want, and if he's up for paying for the extras I want to be prepared. But he seems to understand and tells the butler to leave the case in the bedroom. I haven't seen it yet. I don't know if it's a four-poster or not, cos if it is he'll definitely want some of the extras. The johns who book a four poster always do.

I almost crack up when he says, 'Thank you for coming.' I mean I haven't even started, and it'll be him, not me. Though he might think it's me. But I can give as good as I get when it comes to banter. There's a confused look on his face and he turns his head away briefly, glances down when I say, 'The pleasure's all mine.' Is he embarrassed? I hope he doesn't turn into one of those guys who has to be "persuaded" to do what they've been planning to do all the time. They're a bit of a pain. You've really got to up your acting skills for them, pretend you really care about them and stuff like that. It's a lot easier with the guys who only want to get physical. It can be a bit rough sometimes, but it's usually over quicker. And no matter how long they have you booked for; they want rid of you if they can't perform again.

I want to know if that butler bloke has been rummaging in my bag. You can't trust anyone. I also want to have a look at my working environment, although we may end up on the rug, you can never tell for certain. But Andrew doesn't strike me as the 'rug' type. My bag is where he said it would be, and still locked. I unfasten it and have a quick look inside; make sure everything I might need is handy. I use the bathroom. As I'm sitting there, I have a look around. The bathroom's bigger than the room I use when I'm working from "home". And it's super clean. There's some stuff of Andrew's on the shelf, shaving gear and what have you. None of it too fancy, pretty ordinary really.

I flush, wash my hands, and go back to the, what? Living room, I suppose it is. And he hands me a champagne flute.

Chapter 3

'THANK YOU,' SHE says and smiles at me. I have to say something.

'You look nice,' I say and feel as crass as the words. 'I'm sorry, I mean you look beautiful, but you look nice too.'

'I can be nice if that's what you want,' she says taking a sip from her champagne. 'This is good. Is it what you want? Me to be nice? Or I can be naughty if you'd prefer.'

She looks at me, the question in her face as well as her words.

'I'm not sure what I want. Except dinner. I don't know about you, but I'm feeling hungry. I hope you've brought an appetite with you.'

'I can eat. I've had nothing since lunch, and it was only a few crackers.'

'Let's look at the menu, shall we?'

She picks up the menus from the table set by the window and takes them to the couch.

'Why don't we sit here, we can look at them together,' she pats the seat next to her. I feel like I'm living a cliche. This young woman is flirting with me, yet she can't be seriously attracted to me; I'm at least thirty, maybe forty years older than her. Perhaps she thinks she's supposed to.

I sit next to her, leaving a respectful gap between us, which she immediately fills by shuffling over until her thigh is against mine. She put the menu on our two adjoining knees, opens her hand and leaves it on my thigh. It's all going too fast. I don't want this to be happening now.

'So, what do you fancy?' she says. 'You know this isn't the only menu on offer tonight. And the other one is at least as extensive.' She browses the Corcorran's dinner menu slowly, brushing my thigh with each page turn.

'I've seen enough to know what I'd like to eat,' I say, standing. 'Please, take your time. We're not in a hurry, after all.'

She looks up at me, head tilted to one side, as if measuring my height. 'I can choose now,' she says. 'But I don't want to eat the same as you, it will spoil the fun.'

I must look confused because she carries on.

'You know, the fun of sharing, of tasting each other's meal. Or don't you want to do that?'

My mind goes back to the last time I had dinner out with my wife. Yes of course we used to share like that, have a nibble of each other's courses, see who had made the best choice. But it's been years since that happened. I'm not sure if I want to share food with Georgia. A good name. It suits her, has power and yet also femininity. She's waiting for a reply, I blurt one out.

'I've chosen the crab compote and the venison,' I say. 'I hope you didn't want one of those. I can change my mind.'

'No, no. I thought you might have had the oysters.' She laughs.

It takes me a while to understand, but eventually I cotton on and laugh along with her.

HE SEEMS NERVOUS. Doesn't know where to put himself. I almost feel sorry for him, but only almost. There's nothing to feel sorry about if he can afford a suite and me. And what's with all the 'nice' stuff. Is that a hint he really wants something a bit darker. I've brought some kit with me if he needs that. We'll find out later.

At least he knows he wants some food. I'm starving, but I'm not going to let him know. Don't let them have any power over you, that's the first rule in my line of work. You can let them think they have, imagine they're in control, as long as you keep the edge, something up your sleeve. Like the fake hinges on the handcuffs, or the see through blindfold. Although whether we'll get to play with those I'm beginning to doubt. It feels like he doesn't know what he's doing. I guess he's a first timer so I have to take the lead. Which I do, of course, by getting him to sit next to me. I almost have to pull him onto the couch to get him close enough to touch. Isn't he supposed to want me to, isn't it what he's paying for?

'Come on, sit down here, we can choose together,' I say. He leaves about a yard between us when he eventually sits. Christ, sometimes I feel like a dentist. I edge up close. Is there something wrong with this guy? He has booked, he's paid the deposit, why's he so stand-offish. I try and make it plain for him. We don't have to eat; we can just get down to it if he wants.

Then he gets up doesn't he. As if I've got something he might catch. But he wants to have dinner with me. I'm not sure of the game he's playing, so I tell him if he wants to do the sharing thing, he needs to tell me what he's having so I can choose different. I figure he'll back out, not want to share if he thinks I'm untouchable. He thinks about it a while before telling me. I'm surprised. I thought he was going to be clinical about it. But no, it seems he wants the full "Girl Friend Experience". Well, I'm up for that. It's usually more friendly and easier on the body than some sort of extreme roleplay thing. I get to dress comfortably.

I make a little joke. It takes him a minute before he gets it. I hope he's not stupid, I'll be bored all evening feigning interest in the uninteresting. They've been some of the longest evenings I've ever had. But he laughs eventually, so there must be one or two grey cells working in there.

Chapter 4

'VERY GOOD, SIR, madam. It will take chef a little while. About half an hour before the first course will be ready. In the meantime, can I get you anything else?' says Banks after I've given him the dinner order.

'Half an hour, we've time for a cocktail before dinner, if you'd like one, Georgia?'

She pauses before answering. Half a bottle of champagne still sits in the ice bucket.

'I can stopper the champagne for later, if you wish, sir,' says Banks.

He's good. He knows what Georgia is thinking before I even notice.

'I don't drink a lot when...' she begins, then

realises what she's saying. 'I'm just not sure.'

'I'm having one. I'm going to the European Bar and have one there.'

'An excellent choice, sir. They have a comprehensive list of cocktails. I can notify you when dinner is ready if you wish,' says Banks.

'Thank you, Banks. That will be all now. And we'll have dinner at eight thirty.'

'Very good sir,' he glances at his watch. 'Dinner in an hour.'

And Banks leaves silently. I'm getting the hang of having a butler. I could get used to one. Couldn't afford it though. I turn to Georgia. 'You will accompany me to the bar, won't you?'

'Yes, of course I will. I'm just a bit surprised. My… people don't normally ask me out in public.'

'Why ever not? You're a beautiful woman, it will be a pleasure to spend an hour in the bar with you. Come on.'

He calls in his butler and orders dinner. Then he throws me right off balance. I'm so surprised I can hardly speak and almost make a fool of myself. But I catch myself in time. Stop blurting out the bleeding obvious. He only wants to take me to the bar for a cocktail doesn't he. He doesn't seem to realise all the hotel staff will know who I am… what I am. I've been here before. Someone's going to recognise me. I don't care about that. I'm getting paid aren't I. But if the old guy is embarrassed by it, he might leave some sort of bad review for me, and you know how life is these days. Bad reviews mean bad business. I've had to change my working name before when someone left a bad review and bookings began to dry up. Had to rebuild my reputation and everything. And all because he wanted to go beyond the limits we'd agreed. You can't really trust any of these punters.

But I don't know, he seems regular enough. I can't let him be such an idiot.

'Look,' I say, 'People will see you, an older bloke, with me, a younger woman, and put two and two together. They'll laugh at us behind our backs, and when we've left.'

'You might be my daughter, you're young enough,' he says.

'But I'm not. And would your daughter wear this outfit to go out with her father?' I say, but I don't even know if he has a daughter, or a wife, or kids at all. He hasn't told me anything about himself. But that's his right, I haven't told him anything about me either.

'To be honest,' he says, 'I don't care what they think. If there's a problem it's not me, or you, that has it.'

'Okay, let's go, if you're sure it's what you want,' I say.

'It is.'

Chapter 5

Sʜᴇ ᴛᴀᴋᴇs ᴀ small clutch bag with her. It has a chain as a strap, gold coloured. As we walk the corridor, through the thick Wilton, she slips her arm in mine. I almost recoil it is so unexpected. No one has done that for years. I turn to look at her and she's watching my response. I begin to colour.

'I'll take my arm away if you want, but it might look even stranger if we walk into the bar together, but sort of not together.'

I can smell her hair. The scent of it wafts above her and she's right next to me. It smells exotic, but I know nothing about women's hair. I can see it too. The blond streaked hair has one or two roots of a darker, plainer hue. But I don't mind that.

When we get to the lift, I use pressing the call button as an excuse to disentangle my arm from her. She doesn't say anything, but I think a frown almost forms on her face before she covers it. The lift doors open, and I do the gentlemanly thing and gestured her in first. As I follow, I can't help seeing our reflections in the mirror on the back wall of the lift. Perhaps it's the reversed image a mirror provides that allows me to, but I begin to see what she means. Her lipstick is a fraction brighter than it could be, her heels a little too high, her cleavage over-revealing, the clutch bag too garish. It's subtle, but it's all there. None of her is understated, and much over. I can easily imagine her being judged. She was aware of this before we left the room, provided me with plenty of opportunity to back out of being seen in public with her, if the European Bar of the exclusive Corcorran hotel could be regarded as public. It tells me much about her character and strengthens my resolve to spend time with her in the bar.

I see her watching me and smile at her. This time I take her arm in mine. 'Come on, we'll enjoy seeing who treats us well and who doesn't,' I say as the lift doors ping open.

I TAKE A bag with me. I always do wherever I am. It's got my phone in it and a pepper spray. It has some make-up and stuff in there too, but they aren't important. You just never know when you're out do you? And although Andrew, seems okay, it might not be him I need to deal with.

He almost jumps out of his skin when I take his arm as we stroll along the corridor. Isn't it what he expects his women friends to do? I tell him why we should link arms, but he pulls his away from me as soon as he can, by the lift. I can't make him out; one moment he's all stiff and starchy and shy, the next he invites me to the bar, then he doesn't want to be touched. It's making me feel a bit weird. Maybe I shouldn't have taken the job, maybe… but I don't want to think down that path. Once you start doing that in my line of work you get paralysed because, well let's face it, anyone of my clients could be a murderer, and I'll not find out until it's too late. So I don't think about it. I take all the precautions I can. Hence the pepper spray.

When we're getting in the lift, he looks at me, in the mirror. It's a long look. Now, I've had long looks before, many times, and they're usually undressing me and doubtless taxing the imagination of the looker. But this look is different. It's not like he's undressing me, it's more like he's seeing me for who I am for the first time. I begin to worry, because if he doesn't know who I am and what I do by now, what does he think this whole performance has been about?

Then he smiles at me. It's a warm, real smile. Not a polite smile. And his whole face changes and his eyes crinkle with even more lines than they had before. He takes my arm and pulls me next to him as the lift doors open and we head to the bar. He doesn't seem to care what anybody might think of us being together. I like that.

Chapter 6

Georgia laughs when I ask if she's ever been in a cocktail bar before. It's a deep, throaty, unguarded laugh. She turns to me wearing a genuine smile.

'Are you serious? This is London. Of course I've been to cocktail bars. I've never been in here though. First time for me.'

'It's just that, I've never… I mean I've been in plenty of pubs and ordinary hotel bars and restaurants, but I've never been in a cocktail bar before. I've never even had a cocktail. It's usually beer for me, or a good whisky.'

'You're joshing me, aren't you? Really? Well this looks like a swanky place so we should get a decent drink. It'll be expensive though.'

'I don't mind about the money; I just don't know which drink to order. I don't want to get drunk in here before we eat.'

'We'll be fine if we only have one, come on.'

And she tugs my arm as we sail through the double doors. One other couple occupy a table in the room and a lone man sits at the bar.

A waiter sees us and heads our way.

'Don't take a seat at the bar,' whispers Georgia in my ear,' they're always uncomfortable.'

'Good evening sir, madam. Would you like a bar stool or a table?'

'A table, I think,' I say, and smile at Georgia.

'If you wish to be discreet, sir, there are booths off the main room.' He indicates a couple of alcoves in the room and waits expectantly.

'I'd like a table in the bar, perhaps this one.' I walk with Georgia still on my arm to a nearby table which gives a good view of the whole room.

'Menus are here, sir,' he says, pointing. 'I'll be back to take your order in a moment. Are you resident or would you like to deposit a card?'

I give him the room number and he scuttles off to do something with the till.

The menu is long, and I have no idea what any of it means. But Georgia has already decided.

'I'll have a Mojito,' she says.

'Is it good?'

'Should be here. I like them even in cheap

places.'

'Maybe I'll have one as well.'

'You don't want a Mojito.'

'Don't I?"

'No, it's a woman's drink really, although Jamie wouldn't like me saying that. He loves them.'

Who's Jamie? Springs into my head. I don't think she meant to say it, she's looking a bit embarrassed for the first time since we met. She starts to explain but I tell her not to bother and instead focus on the knotty problem of which cocktail I should have.

'An Old-Fashioned, that's what you should have. You'll enjoy it. It's got whisky in it.'

'What's in a Mojito?

'Rum.'

I CAN'T BELIEVE he's never been to a cocktail bar. I mean, who hasn't in the twenty-first century. It's one place where troubles can be forgotten for a while at least. Andrew must be the most naive old guy I've ever met. I can see him heading for the bar and sitting on those awful stools. I'm sure they're designed to make you drink quicker, and if you do, they get very easy to fall off. And the staff listen to everything you say to each other. I give him a prompt before the waiter arrives and he takes it.

Andrew insists on us sitting in the middle of the room. There aren't many people to see us, not when we first get here, but still, we could have been private in one of those little nooks. It's as if he's proud to be seen with me. It's a strange feeling, that one. It makes me both a bit gooey when I think of the lengths some of my punters have gone to avoid this very thing; but I'm getting all suspicious wondering why he wants to do it, embarrass himself by being seen with me. Is he wanting an alibi or something. But maybe I'm reading too much into it. It's a drink, that's all. And he puts the bill on the room tab, so all the staff will know where I'm spending the evening. They all know what's going on. But he doesn't seem to care.

He says he's never had a cocktail before. I don't mean to laugh, but I do. I'm not really laughing at him, I'm laughing at the situation, and his innocence. So I order my favourite, a Mojito, and he says he'll have one, but I put him off.

I'm so stupid how could I have said that, mentioned Jamie right in front of him. It's the golden rule, never mention another man when you're with a client. You're there for them alone and no one else exists during the time they've paid for.

I'm going to apologise, I'm about to tell him Jamie's my brother or something. But he stops me.

'What's most important here,' he says, 'is finding at least one of these thousands of drinks I might like.'

I say he should have an Old-Fashioned. I don't mean it as a joke, though it could be, but because he'll like it. He told me he likes whisky, so I figure he'll like an Old-Fashioned. I hope he does, anyway. And that surprises me, because I really do hope he enjoys it, and with anyone else I couldn't give a toss.

Chapter 7

I'M NOT NAIVE enough to think Georgia doesn't have men in her life. It's her profession. But to mention one is unprofessional. But she's mortified. The first time, I think, she's shown me what she's truly feeling inside. I can't let this get to me and push it to one side. Her face betrays her, a look somewhere between panic and shame, but not actually either of those things. I can't imagine her being ashamed. But I don't want any negative stuff around, so I brush it away, and she responds well even cracking what I think is a joke.

'An Old Fashioned?' I say, 'are you taking the mickey?' I make sure I give her a big grin, so she doesn't think I'm serious.

'No, you'll like it. Make sure he makes it with decent whisky. But I guess that's all they have here.'

I beckon the waiter and he's at the table and I place the order. He puts small silver bowls containing cashews and olives on silver rimmed cork coasters in the middle of our table before retreating behind the bar.

When the drinks arrive, hers is in a tall glass, etched with leaves. There's a slice of lime and a sprig of mint amongst the ice and the clear liquid is topped with a darker one. The Old Fashioned is in my sort of glass, short, dumpy, squat. At home I would use this type of glass for a whisky, an Islay malt, with a dash of water, maybe a quarter inch at the bottom of the glass. But this glass is almost full, and most of its contents consist of a large melting ice cube. There's also a piece of orange peel stuck in the drink, I've no idea why.

The drinks are placed on more silver rimmed coasters and a small matching tube holding tiny napkins is left behind with the olives and cashews.

'Well, taste it,' says Georgia after the waiter has left.

I pick up the drink and can smell that something different is happening here. This isn't just a whisky on the rocks. It has a tang to it and when I take a sip I can taste the orange and a bittersweetness that proves a remarkable compliment to the whisky. I've got to admit I am surprised. I'm a bit of a snob about whisky and never want it sullied, never even add ice, only a dash of water. But the cocktail is good, and easy to consume. I say so.

'You have to be careful with these cocktails,' says Georgia. 'There are two measures of whisky in there.'

'Can I try yours?' I say, remembering our conversation about dinner.

She laughs and pushes it across to me.

HE DOES LIKE it, and I find myself being pleased, and it's a strange feeling for me. He takes the drink like it might be poison, looks all around it, grimaces at the ice cube filling most of the glass, and then he sips, the tiniest of sips, then another, and he holds the drink in his mouth, savouring the flavours he's experiencing. I wanted him to like it and he does. It's only a drink but a I find myself becoming all flustered, which isn't like me at all. I never let men fluster me, but he's such an innocent.

'The thing with cocktails,' I say, 'is they're supposed to last. That one should take you through to dinner.'

'If it's as strong as you say, that's probably a good thing. You wouldn't want me falling asleep while we're eating, would you?' And there's a glint in his eye telling me this is a joke, and I laugh.

I share the mojito with him.

'I don't like rum,' he says, 'but this is nice, refreshing.'

'It's meant to be, see how he's put the light rum on the bottom and floated some dark rum on the top. That's a classy mojito. You get a different flavour as the drink goes down.'

He tells me he's enjoying himself and leans in close. I think he wants to kiss me. But he passes my face and whispers in my ear.

'Have you seen the staff watching us through the mirror?'

I have, I'm used to it, but I didn't realise he's seen them. I expect it whenever I'm in public. I ignore it if it doesn't affect the punter. But if they get upset I might lose a tip and then I get pissed with them. I sent Sergei to one bar once, when they'd been actually laughing at some smutty joke they'd had, and the punter had buggered off. Never happened again there. In Chelsea too.

'Do you want to take these back to the room?' I say. But he's not embarrassed.

'No, it's hilarious. They think they're better than you, but here they are working a ten-hour shift for next to no money. I bet none of them can afford to drink here.'

'You're right, they can't. But they do when the bar closes. The management expect a five percent loss on spirits and the staff make sure there is. And there are tips, usually very generous.'

'I think it's bad manners. They won't be

getting one from me.

And he's true to his word. When he calls for the bill to sign, the waiter fetches it on a silver salver and gives Andrew a silver pen. He's about to sign when the waiter says, 'there's a space for gratuities just here, sir.' And he points at the slip.

'So there is, thank you for telling me.' And he signs the form and puts thick double black lines through the space left for tips. I can hardly contain myself.

Chapter 8

IN THE LIFT back to the suite Georgia bursts out laughing. I join in but aren't sure I get the joke.

'Did you see his face?' says Georgia, standing very close, her arm through mine.

'I did, he had a strange colour about him,' I say and set off more peals of laughter in Georgia.

'I thought he was going to burst a blood vessel. But you won't want to drink in there again,' she says, a serious note entering her voice.

'Why not? They do a great Old Fashioned.'

'There might be some "added ingredients" just for you,' she says.

It takes me a moment to understand what she means by "added ingredients" and I start chuckling again as the lift door pings open. We are both laughing again as we enter the suite and are met by the smell of dinner and a smiling and courteous Banks.

'Welcome back, sir, madam. The first course is ready whenever you are. Might I suggest five minutes to freshen up, and perhaps a glass of champagne would go well with the crab and the prawns.'

I pause a moment, but Banks has saved me the cost of a bottle of wine to go with the starter. I guess he'd rather the money goes into his tip than to the bar. I resolve to remember his thoughtfulness.

'Would champagne suit you, Georgia?' I say.

'Yes, that's fine.'

'Then that's settled, thank you Banks.'

We walk through to the bedroom while Banks fusses over the table.

'What a lovely room,' says Georgia and throws herself backwards onto the super-king size bed. Her arms spread out her feet dangling off the edge of the bed, her skirt beginning to run up her legs. She levers off the red high heels she wears with the toes of each foot, in turn. They barely make a sound as they hit the carpet.

'Come on, Andrew, we've time for a quick hug before dinner. Don't you want to sample the nights delights?'

Her eyes catch mine looking at her. She is attractive, very. And she smiles at me, raising questioning eyebrows.

'If I come over there now, dinner may be cold by the time we get to eat,' I say. 'Besides, I need the bathroom.'

'Do you want me to come with you? Some people like that.'

'No, no.' I step into the ensuite and lock the door behind me. I hope she hasn't caught the edge of panic in my voice. But she probably has.

HE'S VERY SHY, Andrew. It's bleeding obvious it's his first time. And now he's gone and locked himself in the bathroom. I wonder if he does that with his wife. I'm presuming here, of course. He hasn't told me he's married, and he isn't wearing a ring. But he is. I'm sure of it. And she doesn't know where he is right now or I'm Sally Bowles.

What's going on? Is he a closet gay trying to work out if he fancies women at all? Or is he just shy and naïve, and feeling guilty about his booking and doesn't know how to get out of it?

I'll find out soon enough I guess, but I'm not going to pass up a good dinner, so I'll tidy up my face a bit, when I can get in the bathroom, and behave myself until we've eaten. Then I'll find out if he wants me to go.

He's coming out of the bathroom now. I guess it's my turn in there.

'You can stay in here with me if you want,' I say at the door. But he's not interested, mumbles something and edges past me, barely touching me.

If that's what he wants, it's okay by me. Perhaps he's keeping a tiger under control, and we'll see his real stripes later. For now, I'll give up trying to persuade him to get on with it and see what happens.

I hear the door close as he leaves the bedroom. I wonder if that's rude or if he's giving me some privacy. I use the time to make sure I smell and look as stunning as I know I can. But I'm probably wasting my time and energy. He feels like a talker. He's going to bend my ear about his wife not understanding his "needs" or some bollocks like that, before introducing whatever little fetish he has that gets him off. I'll have to sit through it, hear him out, act shocked as if I've never come across anything so extreme, so imaginative, before. But of course I have. There's very little in my line of work I haven't come across, though I draw the line at blood, mine or theirs.

Chapter 9

HE'S STANDING, LOOKING out of the window when I go in. He turns when he hears the bedroom door and smiles at me. It's not a lascivious smile. Not one of those "I can't wait to get my hands on you" smiles. No, just an ordinary welcoming sort of smile.

'Come and join me and have a look at the view,' he says.

And as I do the butler bloke appears and pours me a glass of champagne. He tells Andrew the starter will be ready in a couple of minutes. I have to admit, it's a good view. Out over the Thames with the lights of all the little boats moving up and down. There's one with a dinner party on board. Reminds me of taking a booking aboard a boat once. I didn't like it at all. It was before I knew Sergei, I was working as an independent. I'd bitten off more than I could chew, and I mean that to sound as it does. There was another girl there, but there were four blokes. It felt risky as soon as I stepped aboard, but by then it was too late. I had to cancel all my bookings for a week afterwards. That's when I decided I needed back-up and someone recommended Sergei. They wouldn't have dared do what they did if he'd been on the scene.

'Do you like it?' he says, and my mind comes swinging back to the hotel room. I'm neglecting my work. What's he talking about I think, then remember.

'Yes, it's fantastic, all the lights on the London Eye over there, reflecting in the Thames, mingling with the boats. It's beautiful, isn't it?'

'I guess it has a sort of beauty about it, but it's not my favourite kind,' he says.

This is one of those statements that can mean a couple of different things. It usually leads to some crap about how women are beautiful, especially when they are wearing whatever outfit he happens to have with him, or if he's been well organised, he's asked me to bring. That would be my cue to change, whether it's a regency ball gown or a collar and leash makes no difference. Or it could be an intro to how beautiful his wife is and how no woman could really take her place no matter how hard she tried and he would have to settle for second best this evening. Then he'd follow up with some sort of apology and request for indulgence of a poor guilty old man who's about to do the dirty on his forty-year marriage and has specially chosen me because I have a striking resemblance to his wife when she was younger, but not quite as good looking, of course; the implication I should be honoured to take her place, even for only one night, barely disguised. So I do my job and ask the question.

'What kind of beauty do you like, Andrew?' Had to stretch a bit to remember his name, but I've got it fixed for now, until tomorrow anyway.

Is she fishing for compliments, asking me to tell her she's beautiful? I almost do, as a reassurance, but catch myself. Her confidence doesn't need boosting by anything I, twice her age at least, can tell her. I give her the honest response, the one that's in my head.

'Natural beauty,' I say, and realise how stupid that must sound. 'I mean the beauty of nature, the outdoors, the moorlands and fells, the sea. I especially love rugged hills and mountains; they have a beauty that puts humanity in its place.'

'I like that too,' she says. 'But I don't get out to the countryside often. There's no work for me there. But I love the parks, St. James's especially.

And I like to walk The Embankment. I think there is a beauty in that.'

Banks gives his deliberate gentle cough to let me know he's about to bring in the starter before he turns into the lounge. I sit while he adjusts Georgia's chair for her. I've got to admit I'm impressed with the man. Not a single sign of anything other than respect toward Georgia, utterly different to the staff in the bar. I'm beginning to like him.

True to her word, Georgia shares her pickled kohlrabi stuffed with prawns and I share my crab, lime and chili on sourdough toast. Both remarkable starters, each with their own unique blends of flavours and both go well with the champagne.

'I enjoyed the starter,' she says, lifting her champagne to her mouth. Her red lips part and she takes a sip.

'I'm glad you liked it.'

'I did. I don't often eat in style, but I like to.'

'I was afraid you might be one of those people who worry about their weight and nibble a piece of lettuce all evening and nothing else.'

She laughs her husky laugh.

'No chance, I'm an earth sign and very keen on pleasures of the senses.'

'I guess it helps, in your line of work,' I say.

She looks directly at me, her face blank. I hope I haven't insulted her and smile to show her I mean this as a joke rather than a censure. I feel her pause and measure her response; she seems to be putting something aside in herself.

'I mean that in a purely practical way' I say. 'A bit like liking the sea if you're a sailor, or numbers if you're an accountant, it helps to get by in life.'

'Maybe,' she says. 'If I hated anyone touching me, I wouldn't be earning as much as I do.' And she smiles.

Chapter 10

What's all that about? Does he really think I enjoy this work? I know it's a choice, sort of, and I like the money. But who'd do this if they had the chance of doing something, anything, else instead?

I think he knows he's made a fool of himself with what he said. I couldn't believe he'd said it to start with. I fazed out a bit. I'm furious inside but keep my fury to myself. I hate it when this happens. He's no idea how much of an insult it is, assuming I want to be here, that it will give me pleasure. I used to like sex. I got a lot of joy from it. But doing this work takes the pleasure away. It gets hard to separate the things you do with the punters to what you do with a boyfriend. Your head is always somewhere else, making sure your safe, checking his responses, giving him what he wants. It gets to be impossible to let go, give yourself over to it. Instead you act the part. It's destroyed more than one relationship I've had.

I think he's a bit embarrassed. Maybe he realises how crass his words are, but I doubt it. Men are pretty stupid when it comes to understanding what they've done. All you can do is swallow the hurt, the anger. But he's my client and the customer's always right bollocks kicks in and I pull myself together. He tries to recover by telling me I'm a sailor or something, but I'm not listening. I'm busy drowning my anger in the money I'll take from him. He's going to pay for this; so I drop the money hint. And that's when the bleeding Butler comes in. He'll have forgotten by the time the tables cleared, but I won't.

I excuse myself, say I need the bathroom. In the bedroom I quietly seethe as I lean against the closed door. I look to see if I can find anything. I rummage in his luggage, the bedside table. Maybe there's a watch, a Patek Phillipe or something. Or his wallet lying about. There isn't. Looking at his stuff I know there won't be anything classy, worth squirreling away. It's all run of the mill. Jesus, Marks and Sparks underwear, isn't he the romantic. Then I realise how stupid I've been. I haven't settled the money. It's the first thing I do. That butler guy threw me.

I didn't want to embarrass the client in front of him, then I forgot. Even if I find his wallet I can't nick from it, can I? He'll notice when he pays me. Sure, he's paid the deposit by card on booking. But the balance will be cash. Shit, shit, shit.

I go in the bathroom and flush the loo, check my face, my make up. Ready myself for the next round. Why does it suddenly feel like a fight? Because he's insulted you, gal, that's why; and now you're going to make him pay. I touch up my lipstick, try a pout, hitch my skirt, and pop another button on my blouse. I'm going to have him eating out of my hands and take him for every bleeding penny he has.

Georgia dashes off to the bathroom almost as soon as Banks comes in. I don't think I've offended her. It was an innocent observation and I explained it to her. I'm convinced there's nothing for her to be upset about. And she smiled at me.

'Shall I wait for your guest before serving the main course,' says Banks.

'Yes Banks. Thank you. She shouldn't be long.'

'I have decanted the Margaux, sir. Would you like a glass now?'

'No, I'll wait for...' I'm about to say miss whatever, but I can't remember her name. It's just Georgia to me now.

'Miss Stratton?' says Banks. 'Very good, sir.

Please call me when you're both ready.'

And he leaves. But my nervousness doesn't diminish. Maybe I have upset her. Though God knows why. She must get this all the time with the work she does. She should be thick skinned enough to deal with it. Besides, I've paid enough for her to be here. Maybe that's it. She's waiting for the balance to be paid. I check my wallet for probably the fifth time to make sure the money is there. It is and plenty left over for a tip. I didn't think she would want cash when I booked her. She was happy enough to use my credit card for a deposit. But she wants the balance in cash. I haven't carried so much around in notes for a long time.

She spends what feels like an age in the bathroom. Eventually I hear the toilet flush and out she comes as I'm pacing up and down by the window like some lovelorn teenager.

'There you are,' I say. 'I'll get Banks to bring in the wine.' I pick up the pager, but she puts her hand on my arm.

'Not yet, Andrew,' she says. 'We need to settle up before we go any further.'

I reach up and scratch the back of my head. 'I don't understand?' I say.

'It's my fault,' she says with a smile. 'I should have sorted it out earlier, but I was having such a good time with you I forgot. I find it's best to get the money sorted out early so we can concentrate on enjoying ourselves.'

'Yes, of course,' I say. 'I wondered when I should pay you. I have the money here.' I pulled out my wallet and began to count notes onto the table.

'You don't need to count it out,' says Georgia. 'I trust you.' But she glances across the room toward the kitchenette where Banks may be lurking. So I plump the bundle of notes on the table and look at her. She leans forward and kisses me on the cheek.

'Thank you, Andrew.'

She pulls away from me and my hand automatically went to my cheek and touched the spot she had kissed. I felt the oily residue of her lipstick there and wonder if it shows. Would it be rude to take out my handkerchief and wipe where she's kissed? My other hand goes to my pocket to pull it out. But I stop. Georgia raises her napkin to my face and wipes it over where the kiss landed.

'Don't want the butler seeing it do we,' she says.

When I look down again the money has gone, and I have no idea where she's put it.

Chapter 11

THAT WAS EASY enough. He didn't baulk at paying up, but he's gone quiet. I couldn't believe him counting it out. Even told me how much it was, a measure of my value, I suppose. I should be offended again, even more than I am already, but I don't know. He seems a bit of an innocent in a way. But he's too old to be innocent, and I'm not going to go soft on him.

They always get distracted by my kiss on the cheek and napkin trick. I don't want them knowing where I keep the stash, do I? Some of the bastards I've been with have rummaged through my stuff trying to find it. I try not to tell Sergei about those if I can. I have to give him an extra cut if he sends someone out to pacify a client. The threat is usually enough to get them to stop. I don't think Andrew will do that, but I won't change my routine. Trust none of the bleeders is the safest way for me.

I did see he has more in his wallet so if he wants any extras, if we actually get around to it, he's going to have to pay. Cash will be good for that, easier for me to squirrel away. Even Sergei doesn't know about my investment account. Every spare pound I can manoeuvre out of clients' hands and into mine goes in there. It's building up nicely is my literal "fuck you" fund. I figure I'm over halfway to my target, then I'll be out of this business.

But it's hard, maintaining the act. And I'm getting older. I hide it well, I've had plenty of practice, but once or twice lately I've seen clients take a second look when I've turned up. It's true I'm not the age I declare on my profile, but the johns aren't counting. As long as they get what they want they'll be happy. I don't want to update the profile photo either. One girl I knew did that, changed her photo to one taken recently, and her bookings fell by half. It's not as if she's old, only thirty-two, younger than me. There's no shortage of younger women coming onto the business either. But once you're booked and the deposit's been taken that's usually it. Punters don't like to say no, take the hit, and miss out on their evening of fun.

I like the long-time bookings; they earn a lot more. But they are harder work. Especially if a bloke insists on another round and he isn't really up to it. Got to use some extra skills then. I've got some special kit to make it happen for them if that happens. It doesn't feel like I'm going to need it with Andrew though. Or even anything the rate he's going. I'm sure he almost flinched as I went to kiss his cheek, but that could have been parting with his money. I have met the odd punter who thought I should be grateful for his company and not expect anything in return. If they only knew how boring they were they'd be too embarrassed to book. But then, I wouldn't be earning so much, would I? Like I say, I'm an actor, making the poor snowflake feel they're important. I don't get that with Andrew though, if Andrew is his real name.

I GUESS SHE has a hidden place to put the money. I don't blame her. It must be difficult doing the work she does. She knows how to do it though. The perfume she's wearing is enticing even to me. I've never smelt anything quite like it. I can be allergic to cheap cologne's, but not a sign of a sneeze despite my taking a good sniff. I only put on a tiny splash of aftershave, especially for tonight. I don't usually bother. Who would I be doing it for? I hope I don't stink; they say you can never smell yourself, don't they. I shouldn't do, I had a good shower before she arrived.

I suggest we push back the main course, let the starter settle. I say it will give us a chance to chat and get to know each other a bit more.

The pause before she replies seems a bit long. I thought she would appreciate that, getting to know I'm not some sort of crazy axe murderer, or something. But perhaps that's the sort of thing crazy axe murderers do. What am I thinking about. I'm standing there, dumb as a mime artist, and I can't say anything that's in my head. It would scare the poor woman. So I say the first thing that pops up in my brain as we sit down opposite each other to talk.

'How did you come to be here?' I say.

I'm sure her eyes widen as I speak. There's a sort of sideways tilt to her head and her brow furrows a bit. I can tell she definitely isn't the twenty-three-year-old her profile had said. But I'm not bothered about that, she's still much younger than I.

'I'm here because you booked me, Andrew,' she says, as if it's completely obvious and I'm utterly stupid.

'I know that,' I say. 'But I don't understand how you got into this line of work. There must have been all sorts of opportunities for you. You seem bright, intelligent, sociable, attractive. How come you're here?'

'I know you find me attractive,' says Georgia, 'otherwise you wouldn't have booked me, and I wouldn't be here. But that's not the question you're really asking, is it?'

'No, I guess it isn't,' I say.

'Then I can't answer,' she says, 'because I don't know the question you're really asking. I may be all the things you mentioned but I'm not a mind reader.'

Chapter 12

I HOPED ANDREW would turn out to be a good guy, and here he is, just the same as the rest. He's struggling to ask me the question I've been asked a thousand times, and I won't make it easy for him. How bloody dare he. Doesn't he know how insulting it is to ask? Twice he's tried but he can't get the words out of his mouth. All this "how do you come to be here" crap when what he wants to know is why I fuck people for a living. Why it isn't obvious to these idiots I can never understand. At least he hasn't come out with it blunt, like some of them do. He's tried to be a little subtle. But I'm not laying it all out for him. Let him feel a bit of embarrassment. He deserves it if he's asking.

I tell him I'm not a mind reader and let the silence in. Ninety-nine times out of a hundred the johns say it out now, straight off. And I normally tell them it's nothing to do with them and if they want me to go I will. Then they want their money's worth quick because they think they're ruining their evening. I can act real good then, accepting their apologies after feigning being offended. Their guilt usually results in an extra tip. I don't mind the question by the time I get to the bank.

'I'm not sure I want to ask the question, after all,' he says, and gives a little frowny smile. 'Shall I ask Banks to bring in the main course now?'

That throws me. The few punters I've had that bottled the question have wanted to get right down to it, see what they're paying for. This is different.

'I know what the question is,' I say. 'You're not the first to ask and I don't normally answer.' And I can't quite believe what I'm saying. 'But think of it the other way round. How did you come to be here? Is that a question you'd like to answer? Is it one you'd ever want me to ask? I'm guessing not. But if you really want an answer from me, would you be willing to answer for yourself?'

That gets him thinking. There's another long pause. I interrupt it. 'Or shall we get on with why I'm here and go to the bedroom?'

He doesn't quite flinch, but he turns his head away. I wonder if he's gay and he's ordered from the wrong menu.

'Okay,' he says; and I begin to stand. 'I'll tell you how I come to be here, but let's get our main course in before it spoils.'

I sit down again. It seems like we're going to play truth or dare while we have dinner. I begin to run through the different versions of my story I've told in the past, trying to work out which one will get me the biggest tip while he pages Banks.

I HAVE NO idea why I said that. Do I even know why I'm here myself? I thought I had some sort of idea when I booked the hotel, and Georgia. I've been harbouring a curiosity about what it would be like, you know, doing it with a professional, what would they know that I wouldn't. I suppose a lot of other men have the same curiousness. But I never needed, or wanted, to when I was young. There always seemed to be plenty of women attracted to me who I found attractive. When I met Liz, she changed my life forever. I got serious then. We wanted to have kids, but never did, never seemed able to. But we were happy with each other, lived our lives and lived them well. Travelled, both together and alone. We didn't live in each other's pockets, but we were each other's rock, foundation.

We began to get old together and it was still fun, we were still finding things out about each other and laughing together. Then she died.

So why have I come here?

Before I can speak Banks arrives with plates. He smoothly lays them before us, pours the Margaux I ordered, and slips away. Hardly a sound from him, or us.

'Are you going to tell me, or do you want to talk about something else?' says Georgia.

I nearly cave into the opportunity to change the subject. But she's doing her job. Making me feel comfortable, wanting me to enjoy our time together. It was a long silence, from when I said I'd tell her to Banks coming in. Maybe she thinks I've changed my mind and bottled the idea.

'No, I'll tell you. I'm just trying to get it straight in my head.'

She laughs. 'Most men know exactly why they order my company. Why do you think you're different? Maybe if we try it, you'll find out why you're here.'

'We've got dinner to eat, and the Margaux will be good. I may as well tell you while we eat, but I'm not sure where to begin.'

She gives a little sigh before picking up her knife and fork and saying, 'would it help if I ask some questions?'

'Yes, it will,' I say.

Chapter 13

Fᴜᴄᴋ, ʜᴇ ɪs a talker. And the worst kind, a reluctant talker. He wants me to drag out every misery and misunderstanding he's ever suffered and play the understanding woman who'll give him a sympathy fuck and not judge him. I've had a few of these. The first one was easy, I took it seriously, believed he was telling me the truth, genuinely felt sorry for the tosser, but after fifteen, twenty, similar tales it becomes impossible to believe. It's the poor women I feel for, deserted or betrayed. But they aren't paying me, so I act the part and give them all the strokes so they can feel okay about getting what they've paid for. But they're the hardest work. He'll be getting my own sob story too, aimed at bumping up my tip. I've got a few I use. Haven't decided which it will be yet.

'Why not begin by telling me a bit about yourself, where you live, what it's like there?' I say. I take a sip of the wine he's poured me. I don't want to get drunk, but this could be so tedious. And he's right, the wine is good.

He begins talking. I blank out a bit, I've got my own thoughts to deal with, but he seems happy to rabbit on. Then there's a bit of a pause. He must have finished or asked me a question or something.

'Sorry,' I say,' 'I didn't hear the last bit, I was chewing. This chicken is delicious, by the way, you should taste some.'

And he leans across the table to take the small forkful I've offered him, and as he does, he catches his wine glass with his hand and knocks it over.

'Bugger,' he says, and it's the first time I've heard him swear. I suppress a giggle as the rich deep red soaks through the table linen and begins to drip from the edge of the barely big enough table onto the carpet.

'Banks' he calls out. But there's no answer, and I'm secretly impressed. If it was me, I'd have been hiding away somewhere earwigging. He gets the remote thingy while I use my napkin and begin to mop up some of the mess, stop anymore falling on the carpet.

Banks appears like a ghost from the kitchenette. After a quick glance at us he disappears for a moment and returns with cloths and cleaning stuff.

'I'm sorry, Banks. I spilled my wine,' he says as Banks begins to clear the mess.

'Not a problem, sir,' says Banks. 'At least it was only a glass and not the whole bottle.' I'm not sure if there's a note of irony in his voice. He glances at me, but his eyes don't change, no conspiratorial look, the corners of his mouth not changing. But there's something. A little hesitancy, perhaps he's holding himself in, just like I am.

But he's good, is Banks. Within a couple of minutes he's changed the tablecloth, dealt with the carpet, and left us alone, sitting opposite each other. Now I can truthfully say I've forgotten what he said. But it's not truthful, because I never heard it in the first place. So instead I ask a question. It's what he wants. And I want to move things along a bit.

'Have you ever been married?' I say.

I THINK IT'S going well, until I spill the wine. Banks is very efficient though. Never bats an eyelid, just clears up the mess and leaves us to get on with it. Georgia seems really interested in my life and wants to know where I lived and all that. But I don't know if I've told her enough for her to share her story with me. Now she wants to know if I'm married. I expect a lot of her clients are.

'I'm not married,' I say.

She smiles a quick, mouth-only, smile at me. 'That's not quite what I asked. Have you ever been married?'

I feel stupid, like some schoolboy caught out in a prank. I know it isn't what she asked and wonder why I haven't answered her question honestly. I'm not trying to hide anything, or I think I'm not. But maybe I'm ashamed of what I'm doing. Ashamed that somehow Liz can see me, would know what I'm doing. I can almost see the look she used to have that told me she was tolerating me; knowing I was making a fool of myself and would regret it later. But I've always been a rotten liar. Liz could see through me every time.

'I was married once,' I finally say.

'What happened?'

I knew she would ask that. I can feel Liz watching me now. "What are you doing?" she'd be saying.

'She died,' I say.

'I'm sorry,' says Georgia. 'It must be very difficult for you; being here with another woman. I guess you loved her a lot.'

And suddenly there are tears streaming down my cheeks.

I flee to the bedroom as Georgia opens her arms and steps toward me, offering a hug. Once safe behind the closed door I allow myself self-indulgent tears. It's the first time I've cried since she died. God knows I've come close, but never actually cried. I've always held myself aloof when with other people, and when alone filled my time until exhausted.

I wipe my eyes and take a couple of deep breaths. I could just cancel this whole thing, send her away. But it's not her fault is it? She didn't know I'd get upset. I wash my face before leaving the bedroom.

'I'm sorry about that,' I say, 'I don't know why I got so upset.' The fake bonhomie I affect is as transparent as the window onto the Thames, but she accepts it for what it is.

'You don't have to apologise to me. I didn't mean to upset you, Andrew,' she says. And at the sound of my name I feel the welling in me again and push it down.

I watch her sitting there, opposite me, the detritus of our meal cooling, half uneaten. I open my mouth to speak and no sound comes out. I try again, push myself to say something, anything.

'I've had enough,' I say.

'Do you want me to leave already?' says Georgia.

'No. I mean the dinner. I don't think I can eat anymore, and it's so good. It seems such a waste.'

'I've had enough too. Why don't you get Banks to clear it away, so we can talk some more. If you want.'

Chapter 14

I KNEW HE was married, of course, or at least had been. Turned out to be a "had been". But I didn't expect the reaction. Sure, I've had men in tears before, but that's usually related to their particular delectation, and I wouldn't be doing my job if they didn't cry. But Andrew, I didn't expect his tears. Guilt is okay, I can understand that, but he has nothing to be guilty about if she's dead. But I guess the memory of her triggered something. Back to the negative comparison against his ideal woman he can no longer have, I guess.

Maybe he's ashamed about crying, otherwise he wouldn't run off would he. I'm glad he has though. It's given me chance to think. I mean, she might have died yesterday. He might have booked me when she was alive and she suddenly died on him. I feel a bit icky thinking about that. How could he? But maybe it wasn't just now, maybe it was ages ago. I'm going to have to find out when he comes back. It'll change how I deal with it. You've not only got to be a good actor to do what I do, but good at improv too.

I figure his appetite will be ruined when he gets back so I eat as much as I want while he's out of the room. He comes back all cheery, but I can tell it's a front. It's obvious he wants to talk about his wife. What an ego rub for me I don't think, a talker who wants to talk about another woman. Still, after Banks has cleared the meal away, I begin.

'What was she called? Your wife.'

'Elizabeth, Liz,' he says.

'And how long ago did she…' I'm stuck here. I want to say "die", it's the right word. But people are funny about death. They say crap like "passed" or "departed" as if it's only temporary.

'Since she died?' he says, and I'm secretly relieved. 'About eight years now. Actually not about, it is eight years, two months, and twenty-three days.'

Right down to the day. You'd have thought he'd have got over it a bit by now. 'How did she die?' I ask, dutifully. I can feel him expecting the question, both hoping for it and wishing it wouldn't come.

'It was cancer.'

'Couldn't they treat it?' The words are out before I can stop myself and I feel stupid, crass. Clearly they couldn't. He looks at me as if he's eating a lemon.

'They tried. She had surgery, quite minor to start with. And they started her on drugs. But the cancer came back, and she had a mastectomy, then another. Still it came back. It was horrible for her. The last three years of her life were spent either recovering from surgery or relapsing.'

Now I'm almost crying. The poor woman. But she's not here now; hasn't been for a long time. 'It must have been horrible for you, too,' I say.

Georgia was bound to ask about Liz. How could she not? But I never expected to feel so strongly about it. To start with I'm affronted. How could the memory of Liz be triggered by this woman who isn't fit to clean up any of the shit and piss I had to in those last few months. How dare she really. But I'd invited, almost begged, her to ask the question. I need to talk about Liz and maybe that's why I'm here. Maybe it has nothing to do with sex at all but only the need to talk to someone about her.

But that last question is a bit much. Of course they couldn't treat it. They tried but it was no use.

I remember talking to her about it, how sometimes for her the treatment felt worse than the illness eating away at her, destroying her body, destroying our life together. I answer her crass question as blandly as I can, holding on to myself, trying not to fall into the Liz sized pit I've swerved around so many times before. By avoiding her family, her friends. By being the jolly sociable acquaintance.

Then she hit me with that. And I suppose I've never thought about what it was like for me. How much of my own life I put on hold, gave up, so I could be there for her. I didn't resent any of it. I wanted to do it, be there for her, make her life as comfortable as it could be. Until she was gone. And this is the first time anyone has said anything about what it was like for me.

'Is it why you chose me?' says Georgia.

I'm thrown. 'I'm sorry, I don't know what you mean?'

'The photos on my profile; do my breasts remind you of hers?' said Georgia.

Did they? I hadn't thought of that. I remember looking at her photographs, and others. Is it her breasts that attracted me? 'They are attractive,' I say, 'but I don't know…'

She unbuttons her blouse even further, and with her right hand slips her left breast out of a lace bra. 'Do they look like hers?' she says, watching me as my eyes flick from her naked breast to her face and back again.

'Would you like to feel it?' she says. And there was something so totally non-sexual in the way these words were formed, more like a mother encouraging an infant to feed than an invitation to a sexual encounter.

At once I feel like a teenager, mute and stifled with embarrassment; not at the breast held before me, but at my own incompetence. Was this why I booked Georgia; so I could again feel the closeness of a female body, caress the velvet skin of a breast, hold it close, weigh it in my hand?

Involuntarily my arm begins to raise, my hand stretches out. And as it does Georgia takes a step toward me so my hand meets her breast half-way; warm and soft and female. My fingers feel the slight roughness of aureoles around the firmer flesh of her nipple, caught between my second and third fingers.

I let go of whatever is constricting my throat and a great moan of anguish escapes me and I again begin to cry, but this time I let my tears flow, I allow the wracking sobs to rend my body. As I weep Georgia steps in close to me, trapping my hand on her breast, wrapping her arms around me, holding me.

Chapter 15

I'M NOT ENTIRELY sure why I get my boob out for him. The professional me would like to say it's to encourage him to get on with the business. But inside I know that's not the whole story. There's much more to it than that. I don't speak to him in the way I do when I'm getting the johns on. The words are the same, "would you like to feel it". I don't remember a single one who hasn't fallen for the combination of breathy seduction speech and naked peach. I have to own up to feeling something here. Something that's got nothing to do with the business.

I've known girls who've had the diagnosis, breast cancer, and gone through the horrors of surgery and chemo and radio and what have you, and it was horrid for them. It was horrid for me, watching from afar. One of the girls, Tavi she called herself, used to talk to me about it. How she couldn't work, couldn't enjoy anything, no drink, no drugs; unless it was a scrip and there were plenty of those. She felt knackered all the time. I tried to be sympathetic, used to slip her a few quid occasionally, when I was flush. But I could only take so much of it from her; until I started checking myself, feeling my tits every day, scared witless I'd find a lump. It was doing my head in and affecting my work. So I cut her loose, couldn't face her anymore. I heard she died, but there wasn't anything I could have done; I'm not a doctor.

But Andrew, the poor sap, he didn't have that option I guess. Well, I suppose he did, but he chose to stay with her; stuck by her to the bitter end. Look at him now, he's a right mess. Never touched a woman since she died, and now he has the chance he's no idea what to do about it. What am I going to do with him now, sobbing against me like a baby? He's certainly not going to be able to fuck.

'Let's sit on the couch and talk about it shall we?' I say. Not just an actor but a bleeding counsellor too. I should set myself up as a sex therapist.

His crying starts to die down and I feel his head nod against my shoulder. I take it as a yes and unwind my arms. He moves away a little and begins to pull his hand off my breast. 'You can keep hold of it if it helps,' I say.

'No, let's just sit down,' he says. He looks sheepish and goes on, 'I didn't mean to be insulting. It's lovely, perfect. But I don't need to do that right now.'

I slip my breast away and lead him by the hand as if he's a little boy. 'Sit down and I'll bring us some wine over; no need to call Banks. You should take your shoes off, you'll feel much more relaxed; I can't wait to get out of these heels.'

And we sit next to each other on the couch, both with a glass of wine, me with my shoes off and my legs curled underneath me, him with his stockinged feet stretched out. We look like some sort of old couple from a movie.

He lets out a sigh and I think he's beginning to relax when he says, 'Now you know why I'm here. What about you?'

I KNEW I couldn't cope if she asked me about Liz, but what could I do, I'd overstepped hadn't I? But I like Georgia as a person, want to know more about her, so I asked. When I think about it, it's a bit like asking your doctor about his health, or your dentist about her teeth. You wouldn't do it, would you, unless you knew them personally.

It all felt so casual in the bar, and when we got

back to the room I wanted to know her as a person, I couldn't only use her as an entertainment.

So I asked. I didn't see it as an insult, but when she turned it around on me how could I not answer her questions.

I've never told anyone as much about Liz, what it was like, never really showed anyone my grief, even myself. God, it's so deep. Maybe it's time to do something about it. But not now, not here; how can Georgia know anything about this. She's a young woman who sells her body for a living, fakes emotions, acts affection. So now I ask the question again, and after everything I've told her she has to answer.

'Okay,' she says, slow and drawn out. 'Where would you like me to begin?'

'At the start,' I say, perplexed.

'At the start of what? My work in London? When I first took on paying clients? The first time I gave my body for something other than love or desire? They are all different things.'

'As early as you remember.'

'If I talk about these things it will change how you see me. You may not want much of my company afterwards, or even any. I'm not ashamed, but I'm also not proud of the way my life has unfolded.'

'I'd like to know anyway,' I say. 'I'd like things to be equal between us.'

'How can they be when you're paying me to be

here? I'm just like the butler, here to do your bidding for the time you've paid me,' says Georgia.

'Suppose I release you from any "obligations" you have?'

'I don't have any "obligations" as you call them. You've only paid for my time. Anything else that occurs is between consenting adults and nothing to do with money. I can refuse if I wish.'

'But do you? Have you ever refused to participate with your clients?'

'Ha. If I refuse I'll get bad reviews. Then I won't get booked. And besides being broke, Sergei wouldn't be pleased.'

'I can tell you now, I shan't be leaving any bad reviews.'

'I didn't think you would. You're not the type to leave any reviews. But would you like to try what you're paying for before you hear about me?' says Georgia.

Chapter 16

He wants us to be equals. He's either naive or stupid, maybe both. As far as the johns are concerned, every client is the best lover I've ever met and there has never been a man to compare. A lot of them only come for the ego rub, or perhaps can't come without it. For them it's just sex and dopamine, for me it's just money. But he wants us to be equals.

He's not my usual type of client; not that there is a usual. The more we talk, the more I think he doesn't want sex at all, but I give him another opportunity before telling him my story.

'I'd like to know you better, know more about you,' he says. 'I knew Liz so deeply. We worked well together.'

'Have you ever had a one-night stand, Andrew? You must have at some time in your life.' I sound a bit incredulous here, even to myself.

'I have, ages ago. It was pretty unsatisfying. But I don't think that's uncommon for the first time, is it? Even with people I cared about deeply, even Liz. I remember the sex, though passionate to start with, was never as satisfying as later, when we'd learned to understand one another.'

'Tell me what you like, Andrew, what sort of thing gets you going. How do you like your women to behave? You like the way I look, or I wouldn't be here. But I know looks aren't everything. Do I smell all right to you? You seem to push me away whenever I come close.'

'It's not that, you smell fine. It's me. I need to know a person well before I can relate to them.'

I'm beginning to wonder how he ever came to be married at all. I've barely touched him and he wants my whole history.

I turn on the couch so I'm leaning against the arm and stretch my legs out toward him, putting my bare feet with the scarlet toenails on his lap. He can't get away from them, but I can feel him squirm beneath my legs. I don't move them and wait.

'Can you...' he pauses. He wants me to take the cue. I wait.

'Can you take your feet off, please?' he says. It's just too polite.

'I want to look at you while we talk, and my legs are getting cramp.'

'We could go back to the table,' he says, shuffling as if to get up.

'No, it's more comfortable here. You can put your feet up too, if you want,' I say, tapping the seat cushion next to my thigh, now exposed as my skirt runkled when I turned. 'Then you can look at me too.'

He surprises me by making the turn and lifting his legs onto the couch, leaving an inch between his feet and my hip. But my feet are now only a few inches from his groin. I reckon I'll have him soon, before we have to get to the parts of my story I'd rather not tell.

I wriggle my feet in his lap; rub one of them up and down his thigh. He puts his hand on them to stop them moving, doesn't caress them or anything.

'Start at the beginning, when you lost your virginity,' he says, watching me.

I almost snort my wine. 'That far back, are you sure?' I'm thinking of the many different stories I've told about having my cherry popped, all dramatic in one way or another. 'If I tell you, will you tell me about your first time?'

He nods at me. 'Yes, of course. It's not very interesting though.'

'Isn't it? Why do you think that?'

'You're trying to distract me. You first.'

I don't know why, but I decide to tell him the

true version.

'ALRIGHT,' GEORGIA SAYS. 'I was thirteen and he was seventeen. Does that shock you?'

'I don't know if I'm shocked, but it is statutory rape,' I say.

'I don't think it would have made any difference on the estate I grew up. Besides, I wanted him to. It was my idea. A couple of girls I knew had been bragging about how far they'd gone with boys; but I knew they were lying, bigging up their experiences. I decided to find out for myself.

I didn't want to bother with boys my age, they had no idea. I doubted they even knew what to do. I picked an older lad, still at school but in the sixth form. I figured he must be clever because most kids left school at sixteen where I lived. I guess I stalked him a bit after school until he noticed me. I thought he'd be more experienced, being older, but he'd never done it before either.'

'Weren't you worried about getting pregnant?' I say.

Georgia laughs. 'I'd nicked a couple of condoms from my mum's bedside table. I hadn't seen my dad since I was little, but she used to have men friends over. I gave one to him in its packet and he looked confused. Eventually it dawned on him what it was and he opened it. He nearly came putting the thing on. By the time he'd got it in it was all pretty much over. It wasn't at all sexy and it was over in about two minutes. He was embarrassed, probably about doing it with someone so young, and maybe a bit scared.'

'Did you become an item, boyfriend and girlfriend?'

'No, not a chance. He ghosted me for about a week, then tried to ask me to do it again, so he must have got something from it. But I didn't want him to. He taught me all I needed to know; if I was going to get anything out of the experience I was going to have to take control.'

'It didn't put you off?'

'God, no. There were too many hormones battling in my body for that. Besides, I knew my mum enjoyed it. Even heard her sometimes. I figured I had to find someone who knew what they were doing.'

'And did you?' I say.

'Do you really want to know?' says Georgia.

I do want to know. The more I hear about her the more interested I become. It might be all lies, what she's told me, but it has a ring of truth in my ears. 'Yes, I do,' I say.

Chapter 17

'I MAY TELL you about it,' I say. 'But don't we have an agreement? You said you'd tell me about your first time if I told you about mine.'

'It really is pretty boring, a bit like most of my life. Are you sure you want to hear it?'

I think he's trying to avoid telling me. The flick of his eyes away from me. They were fixed on my face as I told him about my first time, but now he's evading me. Maybe he gets off on hearing about other people's experiences. You'd think that would be easy money, but it hasn't felt easy up to now.

'I'm sure I'll find it interesting no matter how boring you think it is,' I say, which is my go-to phrase whenever it looks like a john needs encouragement to perform. Whatever is on their mind I've usually heard it before, even the first-time stories, so I'm not expecting a lot from Andrew. He'll think I'm super interested though.

'It was a long time ago,' he says, totally unnecessarily. He's got to be seventy if he's a day.

'I figured it might be,' I say, giving him a gentle touch with both my voice and my hand on his arm.

'I was eighteen,' he says. 'It was at my birthday party. My parents had gone out for the evening promising not to be back until late. I think my friends had got together to persuade one of the girls to go with me.'

'Your friends knew you were a virgin?'

'I went to a boys school and didn't meet many girls outside. I never knew how to talk to them. I probably felt a bit like your first boy, nervous, anxious, stupid. I'd had a bit to drink, so had she. Someone put a slow number on the record player. Yes, it was that long ago, and she was pushed into my arms by someone else. When the music stopped she said she really wanted to see my bedroom and pulled me toward the stairs. I tripped over the bottom step. Everyone laughed, except her. She knelt and told me to take no notice of them.'

'She sounds lovely,' I say; thinking I would have burst out laughing as well. 'Do you remember her name?'

'It was Christine, but everyone called her Chris, and she was lovely. Someone turned the music up when we went upstairs. She'd obviously done it before. When we got to my room, she stopped me from turning the light on. Instead, she took my hand and put it on her breast. She started unfastening my clothes and I fumbled with hers until she took them off herself. It was all over pretty quickly. I remember feeling amazing, like nothing I'd ever felt before. This wonderful woman all around me. Then it was over. I thought I was in love that moment.' Andrew laughs.

'Why do you laugh? Love is a serious business.'

'She knew we would never happen. When we went downstairs everyone cheered and I went the colour of this Margaux.' He swirls his glass before taking a sip. 'I saw her in pubs and clubs occasionally afterwards, but she wouldn't go out with me, and we never did it again. I was heartbroken.'

'How long were you heartbroken for? Let me guess, until you met someone else?'

I DON'T KNOW why I tell her about Chris, I never think about her. I've never spoken to anyone about her, not even Liz and we were together for over thirty years. Maybe the wine made me talk, or the company. Liz and I had an unspoken agreement not to ask about past lovers. She'd never asked, and I'd never wanted to tell her. But Georgia is really listening to me, really interested in my experience. I'm enjoying her company, her attentiveness. I have to admit I'm impressed by her astuteness. Christine and I would never have got on. She was too worldly-wise for me, and such a free spirit. This was in the nineteen sixties. I heard, a couple of years later, that she'd left the country, gone to San Francisco, living the dream of half the teenagers in late sixties Britain.

By then I was at university, in Loughborough of all places. Couldn't wait for my three years to end. Over eighty percent of the students were men. Sometimes we travelled up to Nottingham for a concert at the student union. Nottingham was known for masses of women at the uni. Loughborough was campus based, almost all the students lived on-site, but Nottingham was in the city. The students had digs all over. It had a lot more character, and history, than concrete sixties-built Loughborough.

'You're right,' I say. 'When I met a girl in Nottingham…'

'Nottingham?' she said.

I explain my student days to her. 'That was when I fell in love again. But by then I knew a little bit more about life, and women.'

'Tell me about her,' says Georgia.

'It really was a long time ago, why do you want to know?'

'You don't seem to want to do what I usually do on these calls so we may as well talk.'

'I don't know how, but we've drifted,' I say. 'You were going to tell me how you came to be in this line of work.'

I'm not sure why but I feel the atmosphere change. I can't say what is different about Georgia's facial expression. The smile is still there, she's still looking at me, she hasn't changed her position, moved her head, looked away, but there is now a chill in the room that seems to emanate from her. I don't shiver but I can feel goosebumps rising on my arms. I take an involuntary deep breath and exhale through my mouth. 'Are you okay?' I say.

'Why do you do this, why do you want to know these things? Are they why you brought me here, to find out about me? You men, with your filthy ideas and your selfishness and thoughtlessness. I hate you; I hate you all. With your pretence of care and respect. Ha, if you had any self-respect I would not be here, a paid woman who sells her body so you filthy men can satisfy themselves. For what? So you can insult me.'

She pushes my legs off the couch and swings hers off my lap so she can stand.

'But what have I said?' I'm genuinely confused. I'd asked the question before, why is she upset now?

Chapter 18

I THOUGHT HE would forget; hoped he only wanted to talk about himself, and I tried to encourage him. But no, he came back to it. I'm furious. Can't he see how insulting it is? Why does he think I do it? It's absolutely not for the sparkling company. I try and tell him how offensive it is, but I'm angry and my temper runs away with me; is that surprising? No it isn't.

I try and push his legs off me hard, hoping he gets hurt, but he doesn't, it's all at the wrong angle to get a firm push. I get up and put my shoes on. I could drive a stiletto through his foot, then he'd know how I felt. I'm losing control. He speaks again, he doesn't understand he's being an arse. I should calm down, but his insensitivity makes my blood boil. I want to hit him, hurt him. I pick up the wine glass. I could smash it and stab the stem in his eye. I've been in fights; I can look after myself. I can't do that; I'll never work again. I dash the last few mouthfuls of wine over him then throw the glass at the mirror above the fireplace. It smashes and a few drops of wine streak down the cracked mirror. I run to the bedroom, crash the door closed behind me and lock myself in.

Again, I'm leaning against the door seething. But now the door is between us to protect him from me, though he doesn't know it. I start taking deep breaths, clenching and unclenching my hands, trying to work the tension, the aggression out of me. I climb on the bed, take one of the pillows, kneel in front of it and beat it with both fists until I'm panting with exertion.

I must stop myself from carrying on this stupid behaviour. Why have I let him get to me? I should know better at my age; not that he's ever asked me how old I am. I wouldn't tell him anyway. I don't want to tell him any fucking thing. I hate him. For some reason I've let him in, into the secret part of me, the private part I keep away from the john's I visit. I need to push him out again. God, he's just some old bloke who's paying me but he's under my skin. I'm angry. I throw the pillow at the bed head, climb off the bed, and go to bathroom. I wash my face, my hands. I take off my blouse, stained with tears and mascara. I look at myself in the mirror. Not too bad. I take off all my clothes and scan my body. I've still got it. He might not find me a turn-on, but any other red-blooded male would; even with the smudged make up. If he doesn't want my body, what does he want? That's when I hear him knocking at the door.

'Georgia,' I hear him call. 'I'm sorry I don't know what I've done.'

I ignore him. I stand turning in the bathroom, watching myself in the mirror, checking out the intimate serpent tattoo. It was really painful to get but acts like an aphrodisiac for the most reluctant clients. I run my hands down over my breasts and stomach to the neatly shaved "landing strip" that doubles as the serpent's tongue. He knocks again.

'Georgia,' he says through the door. 'Please let me in.'

My patience shatters like the wine glass. I deserve better. I step out of the bathroom, go to bedroom door, turn the key, and step back two paces.

'You can come in if you want to,' I say. I stand there naked, facing the door with my feet apart, hands on my hips.

The handle descends and the door pushes open. He looks into the room but as soon as he sees me his eyes slide away, he begins to back out mumbling an apology. I feel the anger bubbling up inside me again. Part of me knows I should suppress it but part of me wants to give into it. I stride to the door, yank it open. He's over by the window looking out over the Thames. I walk over, grab his arm, and spin him round.

'What's the matter with you?' I yell. 'Aren't I beautiful enough? Do I stink? Is this body not good enough for you?' And I hold my breasts in my hands and push them towards him. 'Don't you like these? If these aren't why you hired me, what is it you want?'

I DIDN'T EXPECT that reaction. Now I'm wearing good red wine on my shirt and face. I could do with using the bathroom and changing, but she's locked herself in the bedroom and I can't get at it.

There are bits of glass all over, so I slip my shoes back on and pace up and down for a few minutes trying to figure out what to do. It's typical of me to resort to the practical and I begin to gather shards of glass. The wine glass is a ruin and the mirror's cracked. I suppose it will be on my bill when I check out. Hundreds I expect, for something you could pick up in a charity shop for a fiver. That's when I begin to feel angry. The unnecessary expense.

I do what I can with the wine glass. I wonder about paging Banks. I even hold the pager in my hand for a minute. But no, not yet. I need to talk to Georgia first, calm things down.

Even though I paid for the suite, I knock on the door and tell her I don't know what's wrong. It takes two knocks before she responds. When I walk in, she's standing in front of me totally naked. I think I must have misheard her and apologise before I leave, but the image of her tattoo burns in my eyes as I pull the door closed.

I hear the bedroom door open and know it's too soon for her to be dressed, then she starts screaming and shoving her body at me.

I've never been good at confrontation and feel myself begin to blush.

'You find it shameful, do you? My body,' she yells. 'Well I'm not ashamed of it. There's nothing wrong with this, or this, or this.' She strokes herself in intimate places as she speaks. 'But I think there's something wrong with you. You ask again why I'm here, but it seems you don't know why you asked me to come. Maybe it's you who should be answering questions.'

'No, I...'

'No! Why no? Are you afraid? Just like all the other "big" men who have to pay for sex. Afraid someone will say no and bust your fragile ego?'

'Please let me...'

'Please let you what? Have you finally decided to do something? Well maybe I won't be willing, maybe my time is all you'll get from me.'

'I mean please let me speak,' I say softly. She doesn't hear me.

'What?'

'Please let me speak. I don't think your body is shameful; I think it is beautiful.' I wait. The frown of confusion she wears tells me she's heard. 'Your hair is lovely. You smell wonderful.' She's beginning to calm down now, taking slower breaths. 'And I do like your breasts. They're perfect.'

'Now I know you lie,' she says, but she isn't shouting. 'They aren't perfect. This one is smaller than this one,' she lifts her breasts in turn. 'And they are beginning to droop, just a little.' She inspects herself in the reflection from the night-time window.

That tattoo. I admit, when I saw it, coiling around her legs and over her hip, my eyes traced its route and I felt a stirring. Am I fooling myself? Does my body understand why I'm here more clearly than my head or heart?

'Please, I don't want you to be cold. Would you put something on?'

Chapter 19

I'm ANGRY. I told him; I yelled at him. But he never shouts back. He waits and then he tells me I'm beautiful. It takes a while for me to calm down and I wonder if I'll be leaving in a few minutes and have to phone Jamie from the foyer. He tells me I'm beautiful, but he also tells me to get dressed. What does he want, this confounding and confusing man? And do I want to tolerate the crap I'm going through?

He says he doesn't want me to get cold. But it's not cold in this expensive hotel suite. It's designed for comfort.

He says he needs a clean shirt. He does, the one he's wearing is covered in wine stains.

'I'll be back in a minute, please stay here,' he says, and heads for the bedroom.

I'm left standing naked, looking out of the window over the Thames. The boats have almost all gone and there's no activity over at the Eye. The embankment is lit by streetlights on both sides. There are a few people walking; couples arm in arm heading in both directions and on both sides of the river. There is a group of young men looking loutish and drunken. I open the window and hear their voices drift over the water. The cool night air steals into the room, along with the smell of the river. It reeks of London, of diesel fumes and recycled water, of garbage and effluent. My arms begin to goose. The group across the river see me and begin to bellow and wave. I remember I'm naked and back away a couple of steps. I don't want the unnecessary attention; they couldn't afford me.

I hear the bedroom door open and turn to see Andrew. He's wearing a burgundy shirt. I wonder if it's camouflage. He's carrying a white towelling robe with the Corcorran's logo.

'I've brought you this.' He shivers. 'It's cold. You've opened the window.' He leans past me to close it and is met with a cheer from over the river. He looks at me a little askance but says, 'would you mind?'

He holds the gown open for me, his eyes fixed on my face at a point a little below the bridge of my nose.

'Andrew, if you can't even look me in the eye when you have a question how can you expect an honest answer?'

There's a glance of irritation from him before he looks at me properly. 'Please,' he says. And it does sound like a plea, as if he would be lost, cast adrift, without my compliance. I begin to imagine scenarios if I refuse, remain naked, sit opposite him, spread my legs, begin to finger myself. Inwardly I laugh at the reactions I conjure but outwardly restrict myself to a smile. I turn and slip my arms into the sleeves. The robe feels soft and warm against my skin. I take the belt and fasten it around my waist. The edges of the gown touching where the belt holds them, the gown displaying a cleavage all the way to my navel, my breasts held tight enough to emphasise, but not constrict.

I turn to face him. Fix him with a cold eye.

'What do we do now, as you don't want my beautiful body?' I say.

WHEN I STEP out of the bedroom with the robe, she's standing naked in front of the window. She looks small standing there, shorter without her heels, five foot two or so. There's a vulnerability about her I haven't seen before, and a scar, uneven, near her right shoulder blade. She turned to look at me. Is she reluctant to wear the robe? I don't know, but she looks cold; I can see goose bumps on her arms. But she insists I look her in the eye.

She's right, I was avoiding her. I pretend to myself that I don't know why. I was fine when we were in the bar, in public. I could show off being open minded, unafraid of the opinions of others, willing to listen to her, able to take control. But here, alone in the room, I feel trapped. And yet I arranged it all, asked her to come, paid her; and now I'm torn up inside. I don't know why I've done this; I just feel I needed to.

I wince at her comment about "big men" who pay for sex. But I don't feel part of that group, and I don't believe she thinks so either; otherwise we would have done it, I guess. Part of me is afraid, part is ashamed. Part of me is curious, part excited. She slips on the robe and lays the question on me; and she has every right to ask it.

'I owe you an apology,' I say.

'Okay. Do you want me to leave now?'

'No.' I almost panic. 'Please stay. Can we talk?'

She looks at me, a fierce glare. 'You still want to know, don't you? Why should I tell you? I don't owe you that.'

'Yes, I still want to know, but you don't have to tell me.'

She snorts and shakes her head.

'Can we talk about something else?' I say.

'About you? About why you're here, because I don't understand that at all,' she says and there is still anger in her voice. 'Can we sit down at least,' she says and moves toward the couch.

I catch her arm and stop her. It's the first time I've initiated a physical contact. She looks over her shoulder at me.

'I picked up as much of the broken glass as I could,' I say. 'But there may still be shards and slivers in the carpet and the fabric. Your bare feet.' I look down at her painted toes.

'I don't want to sit here.' Her arm sweeps across the dining table.

'I could get Banks to see to it. We would only be here while we wait for him to finish.'

'Sit in silence while the butler ogles me, I don't think so. We'll sit in the bedroom. On the bed.' There's challenge and finality in her words.

Chapter 20

I MAKE HIM bring the gizmo with him into the bedroom to page Banks. I don't want the butler seeing me undressed, and if his previous is anything to go by he'll answer the pager immediately, and he does.

'You go and see to him,' I say. 'I'll get myself comfortable.' He looks like a rabbit caught in headlights. 'Don't worry, I'll keep the robe on. And order some coffee, strong and black.'

When he's gone, I claim the half of the bed nearest the door. I like to be able to get out if I need to. I plump the pillows how I like them and select a few special items from my case. I check the ones with batteries work and secrete them under my pillows and in the bedside cabinet. I'll have another crack at getting him off, so I can go home knowing I've done my job.

Now I've calmed down a bit I'm bursting for a pee.

I regret taking this booking. I felt I was going to enjoy it to start with, well part of it anyway. The sex is never enjoyable, but the cocktails were fun, and the john seemed to at least respect me. So often that doesn't happen. But then he starts with the questions. I've had them before, but never like this, never so calm and persistent. He really does want to know, and I really don't want to go there. I don't want to remember those first few months when I knew nothing and had no idea what was happening to me.

If I'm honest with myself, and who else can I be honest with, I've avoided thinking about what happened all those years ago. Part of me has sometimes dreamed of what I might have become if my life had been different, but there's no point in thinking those thoughts, they only lead to a downward path. One I've trodden on occasion and regretted it. I'm pretty sure he's going to ask again, and I find myself shaking at the thought. I could swallow a Valium before he comes back, but I'd get chilled, give up the info, and feel shite about myself tomorrow and begin the downward spiral again. No, I need to stay in control.

I listen to the low mumble of male voices seeping under the bedroom floor. There's silence for a few minutes. Then I hear the sounds of a vacuum cleaner, and their low voices again for a few minutes. Hopefully there will be coffee soon.

'WE'VE HAD A bit of an accident,' I tell Banks when he slips into the suite.

I show him the mirror, the wine stains on the couch, the fragments of glass I've collected.

'I see, sir,' he says, utterly unfazed. 'I can vacuum the carpet and the couch, which will take about five minutes. The wine stains will easily be removed. The mirror though...' he pauses. 'That will have to wait until tomorrow. Unfortunately, there will need to be an adjustment to the bill. Would you like me to clean up immediately, sir, or wait until the morning?'

'Clear the glass away at least, Banks. And please could I have coffee for two. A large cafetiere I think.'

'Very good, sir. I'll vacuum while the water heats.'

I could go back to the bedroom while Banks beavers away, but I don't want to. I don't feel ready. I'll wait until the coffee is ready and take it in. I wonder to myself why I'm waiting, but I know why. If I have the coffee with me, we can talk to each other while I see to the press and drink the coffee. I can ask about her life; Georgia might ask about mine. But if I go in empty handed, she'll expect me to sit on the bed with her and I'm suddenly nervous of that. Again, I'm lying to myself. There's nothing sudden about my nervousness, it's been with me all evening. The trip to the cocktail bar was an excuse not to be alone with her. Postponing the inevitable I realise as Banks comes in with a tray full of coffee and biscuits in small wrappers. I never heard him stop vacuuming as I stood gazing out of the window, as static as the London Eye is now.

'Shall I leave this here, sir?' says Banks. 'Or would you like me to take it through?'

After Georgia's comments, I can't let that happen. 'Leave it on the table, Banks. And thank you, that will be all.'

He murmurs an acknowledgment and slides away through the door, the lock clicking shut behind him, leaving me with no option but to pick up the tray and take it to the bedroom.

Chapter 21

THE VOICES FALL silent. I guess Banks has left. I wonder for a moment if Andrew has left as well, it's so quiet. I've had punters run on out me before, but never after they've paid. I hear the chink of crockery followed shortly by seeing the door handle turn. I'm prepared. Ready for him. I'm still wearing the hotel robe, but nothing else. I've splashed a little more cologne between my breasts and a touch beneath my navel. The robe is loose across my chest, but not revealing; I've hitched it up a little so he can see the tail of the serpent. If he's a red-blooded male he'll want to trace the serpent with his tongue; I don't get that vibe with Andrew but I'm a professional, I do these things automatically when I'm working.

'I've got the coffee,' he says. Unnecessarily as I can see he's carrying a tray in both hands.

He bumps the door closed with his backside before coming into the room. Does he want us to be private? Has he decided on some action? I doubt it, he's still got all his clothes on, including a tie would you believe. Who wears ties these days, especially when not at work. He comes over to the bed, around to "his" side, and makes to put the tray onto the bed.

'You can't put it there, Andrew,' I say. He gives me a "why not" look. 'That's a full cafetiere of coffee and I'm only wearing this robe. I value my skin, put it on the dresser, or the bedside table, will you.' I'm talking to him like he's a kid.

He mumbles some sort of apology and takes the tray to the dresser. Pushes things aside to make space and puts it down. He sits on the chair by the dressing table.

'I don't suppose it will be ready yet,' he says, wafting an arm at the coffee.

'Not for me, I like it good and strong. You've got time to undress before it's ready. Unless you'd like me to undress you.' I begin to move my legs off the bed.

There's a brief look of panic from him, but he gets it under control.

'That's okay,' he says, 'You stay there, I'll bring the coffee when it's ready.'

He doesn't move. 'Are you going to get undressed?'

'This is really weird for me,' he says, 'No one has seen me naked since Liz died. I'm feeling embarrassed and shy and not sure if I want to do this.'

'Want to do what?' I say, 'We were only going to talk. But you don't want to be on the bed with your shoes and all your clothes.' For a moment I think he'll resist, but I look away from him, affect disinterest, let him feel like he's making his own mind up.

'There is another robe,' he says.

I sense him struggling with himself, as if it's a really massive thing. I've never had such a reluctant punter.

She's right of course, again. It would be stupid to put the coffee on the bed. And she's right about the shoes. I almost argue about getting undressed because I don't want to, but I know it will sound stupid and petulant. So I put the coffee on the dresser and go to the bathroom, locking the door behind me.

I catch sight of myself in the mirror. God, I'm looking grim faced, and old. How can she do this kind of thing with crusties like me? I realise finally what it is I'm curious about. I want to know why she does it, what motivates her. Is it only the money? Then I'm asking myself why I want to know these things. I could read about it, look it up on the internet. I'm sure there are websites where people talk about it. But it's not real, is it? Like pornography isn't real. It's just acting, saying what will get most clicks, or customers. You can't believe anything that's on the web. But she's here in flesh and blood. And she's alive and has emotions and I admit to myself I like her. I like her for being fiery, for not being a pushover, for not just "doing it", but for arguing with me, letting me know she's human.

I begin to undress. Shoes first, I pair them and stand them in the corner. I take off my shirt and look at myself again. I've thought I kept quite fit for my age, walking, the gym, a bike. But having seen her body, its smooth skin, defined muscles, I see the sag beneath my biceps when I raise my arms, the wrinkles in the skin there, where I've lost muscle mass. Once it's gone it's hard to regain at my age. When the shirt comes off it also exposes the scrag of my neck. If any part of the body is a teller of age, it's the neck. The flap of loose skin beneath my chin which wasn't there in my youth.

I'm wearing a vest under my shirt. I think about keeping it on, it was fresh this evening, but only for a moment; it's bound to show beneath the robe, which has no buttons, only a belt. I take it off and see the hairs on my chest, now grey like those on my head. I hate getting old. What do I mean by "getting"? I am old, and I wish I were young.

I take my trousers off. I'm keeping my boxers on. That's a bit too far for me.

It's not cold in the bathroom, but still I shiver. I realise I need a pee, as often happens when I'm cold. I drop my pants and sit on the seat. I would have stood, if I'd been at home, but somehow as I've got older my control of aim and direction has become suspect. I know from the occasional yellow stain on the bathmat at home and the splashes I find on my trousers that sometimes I'm a bit of a sprayer. I don't want to go back in smelling of piss. I give the old man a good shake and squeeze to avoid any last drips soaking into my pants. Even my pubes are going grey. I wonder if I've been expected to shave them. I don't know why that thought popped into my head, probably from reading some Sunday supplement about youngsters shaving themselves. I don't understand why. I never have, and neither did Liz.

I pull my pants up again and put the robe on. It's really soft and warm. Much more comfortable than my old tartan dressing gown at home. I might treat myself to one. I wash my hands and look again at the face of the old man in the mirror. There's nothing left for me to do in here. I take a deep breath and unlock the door.

Chapter 22

I NEED SOME coffee; he's been doing my head in. I heard him lock the door, so God knows what he's doing in there, and he's been ages. I can't wait any longer and get out of bed to pour the coffee myself. I'm standing at the dressing table, depressing the filter of the French press when I hear the bathroom lock click open. The room is laid out so from where I'm standing I can't see the bathroom door, and he has to take a couple of steps before he can see me.

I feel as much as hear him hesitate when he can't see me on the bed. I wonder what's going through his mind. Does he think I've left now I've got his money? There have been occasions when

I've wanted to do that, but I'm a professional, I don't leave until the job's done.

'Georgia? Are you there?' he says. Is his voice tremulous? Does it have a hint of disappointment? Or relief?

He takes another step and sees me, almost jumps backwards. Jesus, he's still wearing socks.

'There you are,' he says.

'Where else would I be?' I say and turn back to the coffee. 'How do you like yours?' I say as I pour.

'Black is fine,' he says. I'm surprised and raise an eyebrow. I had him down as a milk and sugar guy. His generation usually are. 'If it's good coffee, and it should be here, it shouldn't need anything else.'

Why he feels the need to explain to me I don't know. I hand him the cup and saucer. 'Shall we go to bed now?' I say, and I can't help but put the tease in my voice, just to watch the squirm of doubt appear on his face. But part of me is getting bored of the game. He's too predictable in his clear desire to have nothing whatsoever to do with me, physically anyway. He probably still wants to assault my psyche again. I'm not going to let him.

He's squeezing past me to go to his side of the bed when I notice the tremor in his hand and see the spill of coffee from his cup onto the saucer. He doesn't seem to notice. It triggers a memory. My father, the last time I saw him, must have been fifteen years ago. He had the shakes whenever he got sober. He didn't know I was going to see him in the grotty little bedsit he lived in, with the sink in the corner I'm sure he used as a urinal, and a microwave next to it. He'd sold the fridge, even though it wasn't his. I knew he wouldn't have any money. The first thing he said to me was 'Have you got anything to drink?' Not 'You're looking nice' or 'It's good to see you,' or 'How are you?' He already had the shakes. I told him to let me in first and to sit down. He was always quick with his fists, so I wanted to be able to get out fast. I pulled a vodka bottle from my bag and right away he tried to grab it. I told him to wait and asked where the glasses were. There weren't any, only a couple of cracked mugs. I half-filled one and gave it to him. He's sitting down and I'm standing up. He can barely hold the mug in his hands for the shaking. As he lifts it to his mouth and begins to glug it down I grip the neck of the bottle with both hands and swing it at his head. I don't know if I killed him or not. I think I did because I hit him a few times until the bottle smashed on his head. I've never bothered to find out. I was just glad to have finally taken a little back from him.

I'VE SLOSHED COFFEE in my saucer again. This is happening more often these days. I've googled it of course. Like you do when you live alone. When there's no one to talk to about what you're feeling, about what's happening to you. Google says I have Parkinson's, or Alzheimer's, or MS, or a whole host of other options. But it doesn't talk to you, not like a person, not like Liz would. Is that why I'm here? With Georgia? I look at her and she seems miles away, sitting on the bed, next to me. Her hair long and hanging over her shoulders onto the gown she's wearing. She's holding her saucer in one hand and her cup in the other, as if she's about to take a drink, but she doesn't, she just sits there. Her legs stretched out, one crossed over the other, the gown runkled up her thigh so I can see the beginning of her tattoo. Is that deliberate? I don't think so. She's not even looking at me, not drinking her coffee, just sitting leaning against the bed head, holding the cup and saucer, perfectly still, staring straight ahead as if she's in some kind of fugue state.

'Are you okay, Georgia?' I like the feel of her name in my mouth, the rolling of g's and r's.

She turns toward me, her eyes unfocused, and murmurs something unintelligible, then startles to wakefulness. 'I'm fine, fine.' She takes a sip from her cup. 'And so's the coffee.' She rejoins the cup and saucer, turns, and puts them on the bedside table. 'Now how are you? And why are you still wearing your socks?'

I laugh. 'I don't know; habit I suppose. But it's not cold in here.' I turn like Georgia did, a mirror movement, and put my coffee on the bedside table. I bend my knees in turn and lean over to slip my socks off before stretching my legs out again. I can't help but compare my feet to hers.

Her feet have painted nails matching her hands. The skin is smooth and the toes straight, all bar one. The third toe on her left foot has a hammer deformity, not an uncommon thing. She stretches them and my thoughts about the possible deformity caused by high heels are dismissed. I guess she must only wear them for 'work' because she has no trouble flexing her toes towards her; nor, when I think back, in walking barefoot. But my feet are showing not only their maleness but also their age. A lumpy bunion on one side, a touch of fungus on a nail or two, a yellowing and thickening of the big toenails.

'Are you admiring my feet?' says Georgia. 'Is that a thing for you?'

'I was comparing them with mine, how different they are, but no, I'm not a foot fetishist.'

'Maybe it's time to find out about your thing,' she says.

Before I can speak, she has swivelled herself around and straddled me, knees either side of my hips, her hands around my head, pulling me towards her. Her mouth opening to kiss mine.

Chapter 23

I DON'T WANT to sink back into those years after I saw my father. They weren't good to me. And besides, I've got work to do. Why am I not surprised Andrew isn't a foot fetishist? Maybe because he's a bit vanilla all over. But I'm bored of playing his little psycho games and decide action is the only way to get the night over with.

He's more than a bit surprised when I kneel across his lap. I know because he opens his mouth, in shock I suppose. But I grab the opportunity and lean in to kiss him. I avoid kissing clients if I can, but I guess he's clean so take the risk, which is probably more of a risk for him than me. You know how you take a breath before going in for a smacker, well I did, and of course I got a whiff of the unmistakable smell of old man. A sort of mixture of dead skin and stale urine with a hint of halitosis. It's not the best set up for passion, but passion is always absent when I'm working.

I remember the first time I had to service a crusty. I struggled not to gag, but the threat of a beating if I didn't earn the money soon quietened that down.

I've got my mouth on his and I can tell he's beginning to enjoy it, so I grind my hips while I probe between his lips with my tongue. I grab one of his hands and put it on my breast while my tongue finds a gap in his teeth, then another. Sexy this is not but he obviously finds it so as I feel him filling out in his shorts. Yep, he's still got his boxers on, why does he have to make it such hard work?

When I push my hand down between my legs and into his shorts, he gives out that moan; you know, the one that means "yes, yes, more, more". I've got to be a bit careful here. If I go too quick it'll be over before he realises, but if I go too slow, he'll shrivel back to a few wrinkles. I make sure he's as ready as he's ever likely to be, then slip my hand under my pillow. This really does nothing for me and I'm drier than the Gobi. I pull out a tube of lube, break the kiss and use my teeth to take the cap off. That's usually a turn on for them, they know what I'm going to do with it.

I know she's wearing nothing under the robe and the image of the tattoo bounds right into my head, the head of the snake, its eyes staring down, following the landing strip tongue between her legs. Then her hands are round my head, she's leaning in for a kiss. I haven't kissed a woman for eight years; I'm not sure what the etiquette is anymore. Her gown falls open and I smell her; the perfume she wears prominent, but beneath it the unmistakable odour of woman. I respond to her, how can I not? And I begin to feel the erection I doubted I would get.

Sure, I have them, erections. Though it's solitary, I do still have a sex life. When she pushes my hand onto her breast I feel like a young teenager being led along the path by the experienced older woman. It's warm, soft, giving. And her hips, pressing down on me, rubbing against my shorts. If I hadn't kept them on what would be happening now, would I be urging myself into her? Her hips shift backwards, and the release of pressure makes me swell. Her hand is inside my shorts. I feel her nails drag through the hair and her fingers encircle me and pull. God, I could lose myself in this. The moan I let out is involuntary and throws a cloud of memories into my head. I moaned like this when Liz touched me. I remember giving myself over to her, my mind losing itself in the slow build-up of the sensations she created, until I could last no longer and fell into the blinding darkness. Yes, sex with Liz was good, whether giving, receiving, or together.

Her hand slips away from me and I'm jolted out of my memories and back into the hotel room. I feel Georgia stretching away to her side of the bed. I open the eyes that have been closed since the kiss to see her pulling a tube of lubricant from under her pillow. I remember Liz's liberal use of oils during love making, our bodies slippery and warm. I'm initially aroused further when Georgia uncaps the tube with her teeth, but there's something practiced and distant in her actions, a cool efficiency. I sense no racing heart behind Georgia's breasts and remember I've paid her to be here.

Chapter 24

I CATCH HIM looking at me as I spit the cap of the KY across the room, and I see his mood change. The glint of expectancy begins to die in his eyes. He's remembering some other woman, probably his dead wife. I've seen this before in johns; it can go either way. I give a little shiver and hold his eyes while I squeeze a good dollop of lube into my hand.

I give him my best smile and say, 'Will you snuggle with me, Andrew?'

I turn in the bed to face him, slipping my hand between my legs and leaving half the lubricant there.

I sense a reticence in him, something's

changed. I'm sure I had him a moment ago, but now he's slipping away. I gave up the straddle to get the lube, but now I shift my weight back over him and push my lubed hand into his shorts. I breathe the words that never fail to inspire.

'Come on, Andrew, fuck me now, I want you to.'

But he has one leg off the bed and is shifting away from under my hip. As I grab him and smear lube down his shrinking length he takes hold of my hand and pushes it away.

'What's the matter, Andrew?' I say. 'Am I going too fast for you? You've only got to let me know. You can have anything you want.'

He mumbles something I can't make out as he wriggles from beneath me and off the bed. He grabs two handfuls of tissues from the bedside cabinet.

'Here, take these,' he says, offering me a bunch of tissues.

I'm confused. 'Why?'

'You won't be needing the lubricant,' he says as he stands.

'You might not think I do, but I know my body and I think we need it.'

'I'm sorry, Georgia, but I can't do this,' he says as he wipes himself with the tissues, leaving small, torn pieces sticking here and there.

'Don't worry, I've had a lot of experience with men who find it difficult. It'll be fine, now get back on the bed.'

'You don't understand. It's not my body, I'm sure I could if I wanted to; it's me. I shouldn't have asked you to come here. It's not really what I want to do.'

'I can't give you your money back.' It comes out quick and harsh, not what I want to say at all, just a reaction. This has never happened to me before. Is it how I smell, something I've said?

'I don't expect it back. It was to pay for your time only anyway, wasn't it? I just don't want to.'

What is the matter with him? He books me ages in advance, wines and dines me, has me naked in the bed, and then turns me down. Has he any idea how insulting it is? I feel myself going cold inside. I close my eyes for a moment and take a breath, recover control. When I open them, I look at the old man in front of me.

'I owe you an apology, Georgia,' he says. 'It's nothing to do with you. I couldn't have asked for a more beautiful and thoughtful companion.'

I'm dumbstruck. He must be lying. He can't have forgotten the mirror or my shouting.

'I thought this is what I wanted, maybe needed would describe it better. But as the evening went on, well, you know how nervous I've been. I'm not worried about performing, it's not that. It's how I'd feel, about myself, not about you. I have enormous respect for you. But it's my feelings about life and what relationships are for.'

He's feeling guilty but God knows why if his wife's dead. A thought springs into my head; has he been lying to me? Is his wife really dead? But I dismiss it.

'If you want to let it spoil your evening that's not my problem. I can't assuage your guilt,' I say.

SHE'S RIGHT. I do feel guilty. There's no one I'm betraying so why do I feel this way? I search my head to find a reason. It's obvious when I see it.

'It's not about you, or what me might do, or have done, together. It's about me. I should never have followed up on this stupid idea.'

'Other people I see don't think it's stupid. But other people know what they want and aren't hung up about it. I need a shower.' Georgia swings her legs off the bed and goes to the bathroom. She takes her bag with her and locks the door.

I hear Georgia running the shower. The bed smells of her, of her perfume, her body. This is not unpleasant. If I'd been younger I could have been attracted to this woman, I obviously was attracted to her.

I want to get dressed, but I need a shower too. I wipe myself with the tissues before dumping them in a bin, then tie the hotel robe tightly around me, pulling the lapels in, covering as much of myself as I can. I begin gathering the few possessions I have ready to pack, but I can't get my shaving kit and stuff from the bathroom.

I feel stupid. I shouldn't have undertaken this fool's errand.

The shower stops. There's a long wait before Georgia opens the bathroom door and steps out. She's dressed, her hair wrapped in a towel her feet still bare. She avoids looking at me and doesn't speak. Georgia sits at the dressing table, pushes my things to one side and rummages in the drawer for the hair dryer.

I go and shower. I dress in the privacy of the bathroom, relief beginning to seep into my mind. When I return Georgia is sitting at the dressing table, applying make-up, her long hair now dry and fastened behind her.

'I guess you won't be needing me here anymore,' she says.

It's one of those impossible statements. I never did need her, I only thought I wanted her here. But it's not the words that communicate, it's the chill in the air, and her voice.

'You're free to go whenever you want,' I say, at once regretting my pomposity.

'I know that. I always have been.' She takes a phone out of her bag and with a practised hand, swipes it, and keys a number; it's answered immediately.

She tilts her head to meet my gaze as she talks. 'Hi Jamie. It's me. I'm done here.' Pause. 'Ten minutes is fine, back entrance, you know it? Good.' She ends the call. 'Just time for me to pack my stuff and I'll be out of your way,' she says, still looking straight in my eyes.

Chapter 25

'I'll get Banks to see you down to the door,' says Andrew.

'There's no need, I can find the way.'

'It's 4am, Georgia. Hotel security may be curious.'

I think about this. I couldn't care less what the security people think of me, but I don't want to have to talk to them. 'Okay, call him,' I say.

I stand by the window while he contacts the butler. I can see the lights across the river. I hear Andrew muttering into the phone but can't make out the words; I don't care what he's saying. There's a greyness to the sky heralding dawn. My phone pings. It's Jamie, he's arrived. I'm not staying any longer and pick up my bag.

Banks arrives before I get to the door of the suite.

'May I carry your bag for you, madam,' he says; his voice hushed to suit the hour.

I put the bag down and let him pick it up and lead the way. The john looks at me. A small, pleading look, but he doesn't say anything. He takes half a pace towards me, his arms beginning to spread, his body preparing for one of those pretend half hugs people do when they are saying goodbye. I don't want him to touch me again and turn away to follow Banks to the door. He holds it open for me and I'm in the corridor without a glance backward.

Banks makes no attempt at small talk as the lift descends to the lower ground floor, reserved for service staff, which I guess I am, sort of.

'Through here, madam,' he says opening a door to a small lobby at the back of the hotel. There's a night porter at a tiny desk.

The porter begins to rise from his seat to speak to me but stops before making a sound. Probably some signal from Banks behind me. The porter flicks a switch on his desk and the door lock clicks. Banks strides over with my bag and holds the door open for me. I wonder if he's as pleased to see me gone as I am to get out.

Jamie is waiting for me. He has his cap on, the car engine ticking over. It's the Mercedes again. Jamie gets out of the car, opens the back door for me, and collects my bag from Banks.

'Good morning, madam. Have a safe journey,' says Banks, ushering me from the building.

I breathe the morning air deep into my lungs as I stride towards the car, my heels clacking loud amongst the early morning sounds of the city. Jamie puts my bag in the boot. When I'm seated he closes my door. I feel worn out. Not in the usual well-used body worn out way I often get these days, but mentally worn out, like it's difficult to think.

As we drive away Jamie says, 'You going to give me a score?'

It's a game we often play after a gig. One is utterly horrible while ten means easy and interesting.

'Five,' I say, without thinking.

'Pretty boring then?' says Jamie, making good time through the quiet early morning streets.

'Yes,' I say. 'Pretty boring.'

BY THE TIME Banks returns I'm packing.

'Did she get away alright,' I say.

'Yes, sir. Her driver was waiting when we got to the door.'

'Good. I'm going as well, Banks. There's a train at 5am I can catch if I get a move on.'

'Would you like me to help you pack, sir?'

'No, I don't have much to deal with. If you can arrange a cab for me and have reception get the bill ready that would help.'

I cram my few possessions into my bag while Banks goes to the lounge and uses his persuasive voice on reception and the taxi firm.

When I finish packing I take an envelope from the hotel's stationery, scribble Banks name on the front, and stuff some notes from my wallet inside. But what to do with it? I can't hand it to him, that would be crass. I leave it on my case after I've finished packing.

'The taxi will arrive any moment, sir. And reception has your bill prepared,' says Banks as I walk into the lounge. 'Shall I collect your bag?'

'Thank you, Banks,' I say as I survey the room with its still smashed mirror.

He returns carrying my bag in his right hand, meets my eyes, gives a slight nod of his head in thanks, and taps his chest pocket. 'I'll see you to the taxi, if I may sir,' he says.

In the lift I thank him for his diligence while the lift silently descends.

'There have been adjustments added to the bill, I'm afraid,' he says.

I produce a credit card at reception to pay the inflated bill.

'Thank you, sir,' says the man at reception. 'I'm sure you enjoyed your stay at the Corcorran.' He's looking right at me when he says this, his mouth turned up in a half-smile, his eyes blank and cold.

I look away and hear him exhale. It wasn't a question, not "did you enjoy your stay?", nor "was everything satisfactory?", as you might expect from a hotel. I don't respond. There's nothing to say.

The receptionist pushes my receipt across the desk, and I take it. As I turn to the door the receptionist says, 'Do come again, sir.' He seems to emphasise the word "come" slightly, but not enough for me to remark on; not that I would want to, I just want to leave.

Banks leads the way to the door, carrying my case. He walks out with me and puts the bag into the boot of the waiting taxi.

'Thank you for everything, Banks,' I say as he opens the door for me.

'You're welcome, sir,' he says, but his face is already blank, as if I've already left and he's preparing for his next guest.

It's all just a charade. As I pull the cab door closed I remember I need to mow the lawn.

About the Author

Rik Lonsdale's lifelong desire to write had been held in check through three previous careers and the raising of children. Eventually he was able to turn his energies to learning the art and craft of writing.

Water and Blood, his first novel published in March 2023, was inspired by his concern for the future of civilisation and the human race.

Morsels of Life, his first collection of short stories, shares his love of people, their humour, and humanity and was published in November 2023.

Rik lives in Dorset, UK. When he isn't writing you can probably find him at the bottom of his garden tending his vegetable plot.

If you would like to know more about Rik and his writing journey you can find him at www.riklonsdale.com or on social media.

If you enjoyed 'Hotel' you can let the author know through his website, via social media, or by writing a review.

www.ingramcontent.com/pod-product-compliance
Lightning Source LLC
Chambersburg PA
CBHW061454210726
48287CB00007B/2505